"Miranda Shaw, are you telling me you're just using me for your own purposes?"

"No, I—" She saw Mike's broad grin when he couldn't keep a straight face. "Do you enjoy flustering me?"

The grin only widened. "I didn't know women still blushed."

"I'm not blushing," Miranda insisted. "I'm allergic to hotshot sportswriters. I can't come within fifty feet of one."

"Too late for that," he told her. "Looks like you've entered the 'danger zone.'"

She was going to ask what he meant by that, but she didn't get the chance. The very next thing she knew, Mike was leaning over, moving his upper torso to invade her space.

And then his lips touched hers.

And all hell broke loose.

Dear Reader,

I'm lucky enough to have had such a lengthy career that I can revisit a family I created almost twenty years ago. It's been nearly that long since one of my favorite stories, *Mother for Hire,* hit the bookstores. At the time, I concentrated on Bryan Marlowe, a widower with four boys who needed a nanny. Enter Kate Llewellyn, a child psychology student, who charmed them all and wound up staying on in the permanent capacity of wife and mother.

I'd wondered about looking in on this family once again. Here's my chance—and yours. We begin with Mike, a sportswriter for the *L.A. Times.* One of his articles, about a pitcher banned from the game for gambling, arouses the ire of the man's daughter, Miranda Shaw. The rest is romance history.

I hope you find this reunion with Kate's boys as exciting as I do. As always, I thank you for reading, and from the bottom of my heart I wish you someone to love who loves you back.

Best,

Marie Ferrarella

USA TODAY BESTSELLING AUTHOR

MARIE FERRARELLA

DIAMOND IN THE ROUGH

Silhouette®

SPECIAL EDITION®

Published by Silhouette Books

America's Publisher of Contemporary Romance

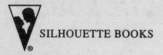 SILHOUETTE BOOKS

ISBN-13: 978-0-373-24910-7
ISBN-10:   0-373-24910-1

DIAMOND IN THE ROUGH

Copyright © 2008 by Marie Rydzynski-Ferrarella

This edition published by arrangement with Harlequin Books S.A.

® and TM are trademarks of Harlequin Books S.A., used under license.
Trademarks indicated with ® are registered in the United States Patent
and Trademark Office, the Canadian Trade Marks Office and in other
countries.

Visit Silhouette Books at www.eHarlequin.com

Printed in U.S.A.

MARIE FERRARELLA

This *USA TODAY* bestselling and RITA® Award-winning author has written more than one hundred and fifty books for Silhouette, some under the name Marie Nicole. Her romances are beloved by fans worldwide.

To Nik, who really did teach himself to read at four because I wasn't getting to the baseball scores fast enough. And to Mark, who is my walking encyclopedia in all things sports.

Chapter One

"Why that sanctimonious, pompous, low-life bastard..."

Born equal parts of surprise and outrage, the less-than-flattering character description leaped out of Miranda Shaw's mouth before she could stop it. The heated pronouncement contrasted with the soothing strains of whisper-soft classical music that was being piped into the pharmaceutical laboratory where she worked.

Her cheeks heated and her breathing became shallow. This was worlds apart from her condition minutes ago when she finally declared herself at lunch ninety minutes after the traditional time and picked up the sports section of the *L.A. Times*. She'd been reading the sports section since she was four years old. Too impatient to wait for her mother to read the all-important baseball scores to her, Miranda had doggedly taught herself how to read by sounding out the opposing teams' names.

Her rabid interest in baseball had come into being because she adored her father. Steven Orin Shaw, known as "SOS" to his one-time legion of fans, had once been regarded as one of the greatest pitchers to ever grace the mound—until a scandal had brought an abrupt end to his career.

But not to Miranda's allegiance. Only death—hers—would have terminated the steadfast loyalty that beat in her twenty-four-year-old heart.

She felt that loyalty flare—along with her temper—as she read words by a man who had been her favorite sportswriter, Mike Marlowe. Oh, she differed with his opinions now and again, but never violently. And, up until this point, she'd admired both his broad range of sports knowledge and his ability to make his topic come alive.

But at this moment, she wanted to skewer him. Slowly.

It was that time of year again, when people around the country packed away their Christmas decorations and frowned over their impetuously written New Year's resolutions, a large number of which had already been broken. And this time of year, the Baseball Writers Association of America turned their attention to the all important question of who, if anyone, was going to be inducted into the baseball hall of fame in Cooperstown.

However, long before the actual voting came the

lists. She had already made her peace with the fact that her father would never be on these lists.

But this idiot, this supreme jerk who had so colossally disappointed her, had the unmitigated gall to touch on the fact that her father had been banned from baseball for all eternity. And he devoted most of his column to the lament that the once-pure game was assaulted now by numerous scandals. Marlowe had belabored reasons why SOS could *never* be considered for placement in the esteemed hall.

It was bad enough to know this without having someone painstakingly elaborate, in rapier-sharp rhetoric, all the reasons that SOS had disappointed his fans and shamed the great game of baseball.

So he'd had a moment of weakness and gambled, so what? Lots of people gambled and her father had never bet against his team. In the larger scheme of things, it wasn't such an unpardonable offense. Not enough to merit being permanently ostracized.

Except that it had.

After reading Marlowe's column, all she could think of was that her father would see it. He didn't need this now, not now. First the scandal and then the awful accident six months later. Those incidents had all but turned him into a hermit. It had taken her years, but she had finally gotten him to come around, to venture out of his shell and start interacting with people again.

This could ruin everything.

The moment her angry words ricocheted around the almost empty lab, Tilda Levy looked up from the computer screen. She rubbed the area just above her eyes before turning in Miranda's direction.

"Did you get your paycheck early?" she asked dryly. It was a given that most of the research chemists employed by Promise Pharmaceuticals felt vastly underpaid, especially considering the demands placed on them and their time.

"What?" Completely focused on the article, Miranda needed several moments to make sense of Tilda's wry question. "No. It's this article."

Getting up from her chair, she pitched the paper into the wastepaper basket by her desk. The basket fell over. Muttering under her breath, Miranda picked up the basket and put it back.

Tilda leaned over, craning her neck to observe her friend. They'd been friends since they'd paired up in chem lab their junior year in high school and Tilda was well aware of Miranda's taste in reading material even though they definitely didn't share it.

Pausing to save her work, Tilda nodded toward the banished newspaper.

"What's the matter, doesn't your favorite sportswriter think the Angels will win the pennant this year?" she asked, referring to Miranda's favorite baseball team—the team her father had played on the last seven years of his career.

Miranda didn't answer right away. Instead, she just scowled and she glared down at the offending paper.

"It's about your dad, isn't it?" Tilda asked.

Miranda shoved her hands deep into the pockets of her lab coat. She wanted to pace, but the lab wasn't made for releasing bottled-up energy of the human variety. It was designed to maximize experimentation.

Blowing out a breath, she bit off one word. "Yes."

With a shrug, Tilda went back to what she was doing. "Don't pay any attention to it. Tomorrow that article will be lining some bird's cage—or sitting in a bin, waiting to be recycled."

But today it was being read by who knew how many people? And, most likely, her father. And that was all that counted.

Miranda squared her shoulders. Bottling this up wasn't going to help. She needed to excise this somehow.

"He said that—" Miranda pulled the paper out of the trash again, holding it the way a person might hold a dead rat they'd been forced to retrieve. It took her a second to find the right page. "'Steve Orin Shaw, SOS to his friends and the players that feared him, sadly embodies everything that is bad and corrupt about the game…'" She stopped, her throat hitching, as she was momentarily waylaid by angry tears that came out of nowhere. "There's more," she finally managed to say, clearing her throat.

"There usually is." Recognizing that Miranda was not about to let this go easily, Tilda left her workstation and came over to her former lab partner. She draped her arm around Miranda's shoulders. "Look, people'll always talk, even when there's nothing to it. And when there is," she added innocently, "they go into high gear. There's nothing you can do about it."

Miranda shrugged off Tilda's arm. Her eyes narrowed as stubbornness came into them. "Yes, there is."

All Tilda could do was sigh. "You do realize that murder is illegal in all the fifty states."

"There's some play for justifiable homicide," Miranda countered. She didn't want to kill Marlowe, just watch him eat his words. And to retract them—publicly, so that a little of her father's pride could be salvaged.

Tilda shook her head. "I don't think a judge would see Marlowe's writing an article insulting your dad as a sufficient reason for your killing him." She dropped her bantering tone. "Let it go, Miranda."

But Miranda could sooner stop breathing than say nothing. Her father needed someone in his corner, fighting the fight he wouldn't. Being banished from baseball had robbed him of his spirit, his zest. Granted, as she grew older, he'd had less and less time for her because he was on the road so much. And then Ariel had died and everything began to fall apart. First her parents' marriage and then her mother. But, through it all, the one thing she wouldn't allow to change was the way she felt about her father.

He needed her more than ever now.

"I can't."

Miranda planted herself in front of her computer again. But this time, there were no equations, no on-going research figures dancing before her on the monitor. She pulled up a screen and began to write. Feverishly. Had they been wired for sound, the keys on the keyboard would have groaned and whimpered from the lightning assault.

Curious, Tilda looked over her shoulder. "What are you doing?"

Miranda continued typing. She lifted her chin as she answered, as if silently daring the world to take a swing at her for expressing her opinion.

"I'm telling Mike Marlowe what I think of him and his high-handed article."

"Are you going to tell him whose daughter you are?"

They both knew that would probably add weight to the e-mail. But it would also make it seem biased. And she was doing her best to be fair—not that the cretin deserved it.

She paused to push her blond bangs out of eyes that turned a darker shade of blue when she was angry. "No, just that he's an ass."

Tilda laughed, shaking her head. Backing away, she gave her friend some measure of privacy. Her mouth curved in amusement. "I'm sure that he'll find that enlightening."

Mike Marlowe had expected feedback from his article. To some degree, he got it with every article he wrote for the *Times*. With his most recent piece he'd expected e-mail from die-hard lovers of the game who agreed with him.

It was sad, really, he thought. There'd been a time when Shaw had been revered as the greatest pitcher who'd ever lived, certainly the greatest living pitcher of his generation. He could make the ball do everything but sing the national anthem—and there was some doubt about that. He remembered watching the man play and worshiping his precision. In an arena where a career total of three thousand strikeouts was astounding, SOS had managed to garner two more than four thousand. A lifetime total of three hundred wins was something every starting pitcher dreamed of. SOS had three hundred and seventy-seven under his belt when he was forced to retire from the game.

In almost every way, the man had been a god among men, *almost* being the key word.

And it was *almost* that wound up being Shaw's undoing.

The one unpardonable offense in baseball was not the loss of a crucial game, or the throw of a wild pitch that ultimately cost the team the World Series. It was steroid use and gambling.

It didn't even have to be the supreme sin of betting against your own team, which indicated that you were somehow involved in throwing the game. The very act of placing a bet where the outcome of a sporting event was the deciding factor of the prize was comparable to partaking of the forbidden fruit. SOS had committed that offense, that one unforgivable sin. One late summer he had bet on a series of games. And he had been discovered and disgraced.

Mike supposed it was to the man's credit that Shaw hadn't tried to deny what he was being accused of or attempted to explain it away. He hadn't pleaded temporary insanity or momentary drunken enthusiasm for the game he loved more than life itself. Shaw had stepped up to the plate, taken the pitch without flinching and retired his bat, as well as his glove.

Mike remembered that awful day well. Remembered hearing the news broadcast just as he and his family were about to have dinner. Remembered catching those mind-numbing words—banned from baseball forever—just as his father had turned off the set in the living room. Hearing them, he'd bolted out of the kitchen back into the living room and turned the television set on again, his stomach twisting itself into a knot. He was twelve at the time, too young to lose a hero to the ugliness of reality.

Surprised by his actions, his father had begun to reprimand him, but Kate, the wonderful woman who had become their stepmother, had shaken her head and told his father to come help her in the kitchen. Kate knew how much the game—and the pitcher—had meant to him.

There was no question that he loved his dad, even during Bryan Marlowe's absenteeism just before Kate had come into their lives, but as for heroes, well, there was only one for him. Steven Orin Shaw. SOS.

That August day—August 7th—he'd been stripped of his hero. Stripped of his innocence. SOS had come crashing down off the mile-high pedestal he and countless other boys and men had placed him on. After listening to the news bulletin, a dark parade of emotions had bounced around inside of him: disbelief, denial, dismay, disappointment.

Disappointment eventually overtook his other emotions, making him hurt so bad he could hardly stand it. His brothers had tried to help him come around, as had his father. But it was Kate who'd finally gotten him out of the tailspin.

"We'll never know the real full story," she'd told him, sitting beside him on his bed in his room later that night. "Mr. Shaw isn't elaborating on what made him do this. And, up until now, he's been a very good, decent man who played his heart out for the game."

"How do you know he's a good, decent man?" he'd challenged, doing his best not to cry angry tears. Tears were for babies. "He coulda done something else we don't know about."

"Maybe," Kate had agreed. She ran her fingers through his light blond hair, the very action calming him down. "But I really don't think so."

"Why?"

"Because there's pain in his eyes," she told him simply. "Deep, bottomless pain. He's had tragedy in his life and survived. Those kind of people are honorable people."

He remembered looking at her then, confused. "What kind of tragedy?"

"His older daughter, Ariel, died of cancer. Something like that can destroy a person, but he went on playing. Because a lot of little boys like you were counting on him."

"Then why did he do this?" he'd cried.

"I don't know, Mike. But I do know that he's sorry it ever happened. Sorry that he disappointed boys like you. And girls, too," she added with that smile of hers that promised him it would be all right.

And it was.

Eventually.

Discovering that his hero had feet of clay hadn't killed his love of the game—something else he shared with his stepmother. He went on to go to other baseball games and eventually, could even tolerate watching the Angels play again. Without Shaw.

Like all boys at some point or other, he'd entertained

dreams of being a baseball player himself. Not outstanding enough to ever make it to the minors, much less
the majors, he went to college, got a degree in journal-
ism and did the next best thing to playing—writing
about the game and the players who made it all come to
life.

He'd honestly thought he'd gotten over his disappointment in Shaw until he'd started writing the article.
It was as if something deep inside of him was set free.
The boy who'd been so sorely disappointed had been
there all along, waiting to ask why.

Until he knew why, he couldn't begin to forgive.
But all his attempts at interviewing Shaw over the last
few years during baseball season had been rebuffed.
The man didn't even return his phone calls.

Every year the members of the Baseball Writers Association of America would get together and pore over a
list of eligible retired players to decide if there were any
viable candidates. This year, there had been a rumor going
around that perhaps it was time to bend the rules a bit, to
forgive and forget and welcome a man who, had he not
committed the unforgivable, would have been a shoo-in.

As far as Mike was concerned, there was a difference
between retired and run out on a rail. One was honorable, the other drenched in disgrace.

When he'd heard the rumor a third time, Mike knew
he had to say something, to finally speak up and make
his feelings known. Looking back, maybe it had been
the hurt boy who had written the article. But what he'd
written needed to be said and he was certain that it had
been the right thing to do.

But obviously "Miranda" from Bedford didn't share his opinion, he thought with a bemused smile as he read her latest e-mail. She'd told him so in no uncertain words—he paused to count the number of e-mails with her name on them—ten times. Ten *different* times. He shook his head. Who would have thought there were ten different ways to say the same thing?

The woman was probably an old groupie, he thought. Baseball groupies had been around as long as the game, following a team from city to city just to sit in the stands and look adoringly at some player or other, if not the whole team. He had no doubt that Miranda had probably gotten a little something on the side once from SOS—the man was only human after all—and felt a personal connection to the pitcher.

Mike rolled the thought over in his head. Shaw had been touted as the ultimate family man—until the death of his daughter. Shaw's wife, he'd heard, never recovered and eventually died, but not before divorcing him. That had been a black period for the pitcher, but he still played. Some said better than ever, as if he was taking solace the only way he knew how. Off the field, there'd been talk of women and wild parties, but nothing had ever been substantiated.

Mike couldn't help thinking that this Miranda was probably from that era.

Straightening, Mike began to type.

Dear Miranda, he wrote. I'm afraid that you might be allowing sentiment to cloud your judgment. No one is arguing that SOS wasn't a dynamic player in his day, only that he turned out to be a monumental disappointment to the worshipful boys—and girls, he added in deference to his stepmother, who all thought of him as their hero. Heroes blackened by scandals are no longer heroes, no matter what their personal stats are. I stand by my position. Under no circumstances is SOS to be absolved of his sin and welcomed into the hall of fame, to share space with the men who truly deserve to be there.

He reread his words once, decided that he was satisfied and hit Send.

Working at her station, Miranda noticed the e-mail response that suddenly popped up in the corner of her screen. Because the subject referenced was the title of the article that had gotten her so angry, she opened the e-mail immediately. She hadn't really expected an answer.

Scanning the reply, she set her jaw hard. Within a heartbeat, she was firing back a response to Marlowe's response.

Were you always such a pompous ass, or did your present so-called vocation do that to you? I've been following your column for some time now. Until today, I actually thought you had a brain, as well as a heart, but obviously the wizard decided to abruptly take them both back.

Not bothering to reread her words, something she usually did very carefully before sending *anything*, Miranda hit Send. She hit the key so hard, she broke a nail.

Out of the corner of her eye, she could see Tilda watching her. Taking a deep breath, she forced herself to let it out slowly in an attempt to calm down. But she'd no sooner blown that breath out than more words appeared on her screen.

Clever. Obviously I am not going to make my case with you, which is all right. Different opinions are what make the world go around. Let's just agree to disagree.

He was being lofty, and high-handed, making her out to be the small-minded one here when they both knew it was him.

I don't agree to anything, she fired back. You're wrong, as well as inflexible. If you were in front of me right now, I'd make you eat your words.

Mike leaned back, studying the latest missive that tore across his screen like silent gunfire. He'd obviously struck a nerve. Part of him felt like just letting this go. But both his father and stepmother had taught him to stand up for what he believed and never to back away from a fight, even one that was annoyingly inconsequential, like this one.

No matter what my location, he typed, referring to her comment about standing in front of her, I'd still believe what I believe. He took off the kid gloves he'd envisioned himself wearing during the initial response. Forgiveness is for dropped pitches, not dropped morals. If you'd like to continue this debate in person, you name the time and place.

There, that should put her in her place, he thought, pressing Send.

Mike didn't think he'd receive an answer, other than a few choice expletives, so he was rather surprised when yet another volley of words appeared on his computer screen.

Bailey's Sports Bar. Six o'clock. Today.

Chapter Two

Mike stared at the screen, waiting for something more to appear.

Several seconds passed. No additional words materialized. The brief, staccato sentences seemed to pulse on the field of white, looking for all the world like a challenge. It reminded him of a cocky kid with his chin thrust forward, daring him to take a swing.

Except that in this case, the words belonged to a cocky female. One who obviously lived and breathed the game of baseball—or maybe just focused on Shaw to the exclusion of everything else.

The woman obviously was in dire need of a life, he decided.

For a second, he debated the wisdom of meeting

her. Undoubtedly, there were too many birds nesting on her antennae and he had no desire to get tangled up with a crazy woman. But then, Bailey's Sports Bar was a pretty crowded place at six, even on a Monday. Besides, he had to admit that his curiosity had been aroused. If the woman actually knew SOS, she might be willing to tell a few stories. This might the closest thing to an interview with Shaw that he could score.

Or maybe, if he played his cards right and she *did* know the former pitcher, he might even wind up getting an introduction.

But as he finally put his hand to the keyboard, Mike saw a single word take form on his screen. Afraid?

She'd hit him where he lived.

You're on, he typed, then realized he needed a way to recognize her when she walked into Bailey's. How will I know you?

Her answer was far from satisfying. Instead of a description, she gave him a cryptic reply. I'll know you.

Miranda liked having the advantage on her side. Maybe it wasn't polite, but at the moment, with the article still warm on her desk, she wasn't feeling very polite. And this know-it-all didn't deserve any cut slack.

Unless the photo on top of your column is an outdated one, she added.

It was a distinct possibility. A great many people in the arts used publicity photographs far more reminiscent of years gone by than of present day.

He answered her in less than a beat. Only by a year.

That meant he was good-looking, Miranda thought. Either that, or the photographer was deeply enamored of Photoshop. In either case, it didn't matter. Giving the man a piece of her mind in person was most important. If people like him, bent on maintaining a grudge, didn't exist, her father could receive the honor he richly deserved. He told her that it didn't matter to him, but she knew better. How could something like that *not* matter?

Good, she typed. I'll see you at six, she reiterated.

Maybe six-thirty would be a better time, Mike decided, typing the words the moment he reconsidered.

But it was too late. The woman on the other end of the dueling e-mail exchange was gone. His amended suggestion received no response and the sentence he'd typed sat as a solitary bottom line, lonely and unnoticed. The dialogue, such as it was, was over.

Mike studied the very brief correspondence, beginning with the woman's opening e-mail to him about today's column. This "Miranda" had to be old, he decided. His proof was that there were no one-letter shortcuts in any of the messages as had become the custom in quick messaging. It was a way of communication that personally irritated him. As a journalist, he'd always thought of the English language as an art form, something to be utilized rather than pared down. Most of the people he worked and socialized with didn't feel the same. They were all in their twenties or early thirties.

This led him to the conclusion that the woman he had agreed to meet in person had to be some obsessed middle-aged—or older—harpy. She probably had a shrine in her bedroom devoted to Steven Orin Shaw, complete with a wall of photographs. Most likely she had it surrounded with candles.

Mike leaned back in his chair, knotting his fingers together behind his head as he mulled over the situation.

Maybe he wouldn't show.

He *did* have an excuse. It was only Monday, but he did have to start getting ready to fill in for Ryan Wynters this weekend. The senior sportswriter had come down with the worst case of flu according to his editor, Howard Hilliard. Ryan was supposed to be covering the Super Bowl this Sunday. Since he was next in line, that meant that he was now covering the tradition-honored event. By all rights, he should be home, packing, not wasting his time sitting on a bar stool in a sports bar with some incensed female nut-job intent on a duel of words.

Whoever this Miranda was, he wasn't going to convince her and she wasn't going to convince him. What was the point of going?

He frowned.

The point of going was that he'd said he would. And he always kept his word.

Mike sighed.

Lance Matthews, the theater critic who sat opposite him, looked up. His gaunt, elongated face was devoid of any sort of telltale emotion or even a clue as to his thoughts.

"A little stronger and that could qualify as a class one hurricane. Did Ryan call in to say he was feeling well enough to cover the Soup Bowl after all?"

"Super Bowl," Mike automatically corrected, even though he knew that Lance had made the mistake on

purpose. Just like everyone knew that Ryan had to prac-
tically be on his death bed to miss the event. "No," he
added slowly, "I'm just debating whether or not to meet
this fan at a sports bar."

Something akin to mild interest passed over Lance's
alabaster face. "Fan of what? You?"

Mike heard the incredulous note in the other man's
voice. Lance was the one with an ego, not him. "No, of
Steven Shaw."

The man nodded and Mike expected him to drop
the matter. Lance looked down his nose at anything
more physical than finding the seat numbers on his
theater tickets. But apparently the man did absorb a
few things that went on around him. He actually knew
who Steven Shaw was.

"They're a small but steadfast bunch. Loyal to the
end, so I hear. I thought they might come out of the
woodwork after your little Steven-Shaw-should-rot-in-
hell-for-all-eternity piece." He ended the pronouncement with a smug smirk.

"I didn't say that," Mike protested. "I just said that,
if we reconsider our stand and put him in the running
for the hall of fame, then we've surrendered our stan-
dards. We'd be setting a terrible precedent and a bad
example for the younger fans."

Lance raised his hand in defense. "Please, spare me.
I don't need to have you quote the entire article for me.
I assure you, I get the gist." Lance paused, then added,
"And, as a matter of fact, I quite agree."

That stunned Mike. He couldn't remember when he
and the other man had agreed on anything.

"What I don't agree with is your actually meeting with this so-called 'fan.' At least, not without taking some pepper spray with you. Did it occur to you that this woman might be deranged? Of course," he added, "anyone who's so rabid about sports has to be a little deranged as far as I'm concerned."

That made up Mike's mind for him. "Thanks for your concern, but I can take care of myself."

The smirk on Lance's lips widened and the theater critic shook his head as if to say, *Poor fool.* What he did say was, "I take it you never saw *Misery.*"

That would be the movie about the fanatical fan, Mike thought. "As a matter of fact, I have. If this Miranda comes into the bar carrying a hatchet, I'll be sure to duck out the back."

Lance's eyes narrowed, but there was still evidence of contempt. "It might very well be too late by then."

Mike shrugged. "I'll take my chances," he said, before getting back to his notes for his next day's column.

And so, approximately five hours later, Mike found himself securely planted on a bar stool, nursing a warm glass of beer and watching the door. But every time it opened, someone other than this so-called Miranda—who called their kid Miranda, anyway?—entered.

His beer was almost gone.

He'd arrived ten minutes before six, preferring to be early so that he had the advantage of observing the woman when she crossed the floor. He wanted to size her up before they met face-to-face. No woman he knew—other than Kate—was ever anything but late.

He glanced at his watch. Six o'clock on the dot. Dollars to donuts, she wasn't going to show, he thought, taking another sip of his beer. Setting the mug down, he ran a thumb over his lips to eliminate any residue suds. He'd give her fifteen minutes, then leave.

When an older woman walked in alone, Mike was sure he'd found his challenger. She looked at him for a long moment, her eyes traveling over the length of his body as if he were a tall, frosty glass of ice water and she were newly arrived from the desert. And then, after a slight hesitation that appeared to be tinged with regret, she continued walking right past him.

Damn, he didn't have time for this. After draining his glass, he set it back down on the bar with finality. He really did need to get going. He hadn't finished his article and there was still that packing to do. He never liked leaving things until the last minute. He never knew when he might need that minute for something else.

Preoccupied, he didn't feel the hand on his arm, didn't realize there was anyone standing beside him until he turned right into her. And bumped up against possibly the firmest soft body he'd ever encountered. Thrown off guard, Mike took a quick step back.

The apology was automatic, as were the manners ingrained in him from a very young age. "Sorry, didn't see you standing there." Wow, she was hot and he tried not to stare. It had been a while since he'd witnessed such a perfect combination of body and face. "My gorgeous woman radar must be down."

"Right along with your common sense, I see," the woman countered. A hint of a smile curved her lips. Or maybe that was just his imagination. "That line doesn't really work, does it?"

"It's not a line," he assured her. Very few women took his breath away. After all, this was Southern California, where more than a preponderance of beautiful women existed, many of whom held down "other" jobs in Hollywood. But this one was definitely in a class by herself. "Just an honest observation."

She looked at him for a long moment. He almost got the impression she was staring straight into his mind.

"Like all your other observations?" she finally asked.

Was that a smirk on her face? Why? They didn't know each other. God knew he would have remembered meeting a woman who exuded what he could only term as barely harnessed sexuality. Her long blond hair was bound up with a few pins. He had a feeling if he pulled them out, like in one of those old, hokey, grade B movies, a storm of swirling blond curls would tumble down and all but overwhelm her face. He usually liked sleek hair, but on her, he would have bet his soul that curly would look damn good.

Almost as good as those curves beneath the sensible navy blue jacket and matching pencil skirt.

For some reason, he caught himself thinking of one of those fantasies, the ones that started out with a refined, scholarly looking woman who, with a little bit of coaxing, turned into a smoldering tigress.

He definitely needed to get out more.

The way she watched him made him feel they knew each other. But how? He would have remembered her, no question.

"Do I know you?" he finally asked. Although it was tempting, he didn't add that he knew he *wanted* to know her because that, too, sounded like a line. A pitiful one.

Miranda deliberately took her time, enjoying that he obviously felt at a disadvantage. Her eyes slowly swept over the journalist. It was something she'd learned from observing her father. With every pitch, SOS had taken his time on the mound, sizing up the batter each and every time, unnerving him as he mentally selected just the right pitch to throw and bring the batter down.

Rather than saying no, or drawing the moment out, she ended his quandary and replied, "I'm Miranda."

Like a drawbridge that had its chains severed, Mike's mouth dropped open. His eyes widened as he stared at her in disbelief.

"*You're* Miranda?" So much for intuition, Mike upbraided himself. Unless this woman had an amazing plastic surgeon on retainer, she wasn't any older than about twenty-five.

Amusement highlighted her face. She enjoyed catching the man off guard, although she wasn't exactly sure why he looked as surprised as he did.

"Yes, I am." Her line of work had taught her to go straight to the heart of the matter when it came to getting answers. "Just what were you expecting?"

The image of a fanatical groupie chasing after Shaw in orthopedic sneakers instantly disintegrated. How had the man managed to attract someone so young into his camp? She was too young to have watched many of his games.

"Not you," he replied honestly.

The words seemed to emerge out of his mouth in slow motion. Which happened to be the exact speed of his brain waves. This was an unusual predicament for him. Competition for jobs as a sportswriter was close to cutthroat. His lightning-fast brain—with a tongue to match—was what had landed him the position at the *Times* to begin with. So just how did one drop-dead gorgeous female negate all that without even trying?

At any other time, Miranda might have been flattered. It had been a long time since she'd found herself in a social position, a long time since she'd been on the receiving end of a compliment. Test tubes and analytical data tended to be silent. But this was the man who had seen fit to mount a crusade against her father. Which made him unlikable, no matter how pretty his blue eyes were.

"Baseball fans come in all sizes and shapes," she informed him and then tried not to respond as she felt his eyes drift over her. His gaze couldn't have been more intense if he were measuring her for a thong bikini.

"Obviously," he murmured.

And they did, he'd be the first one to say that. It was just that he'd had a preconceived notion of what she, SOS's champion, would look like. He'd met a few of SOS's fans, the ones who continued to stick by him despite the betting scandal. This Miranda was far too young to be a fan. And yet, he thought back to the heated e-mail exchange. She was definitely a fan. But it made no sense to him. Most people Miranda's age didn't even know who—or what, for that matter—SOS was.

He realized suddenly that he had completely forgotten his manners. Kate wouldn't have been happy with him. Rising to his feet, he gestured toward the other end of the room, where round tables and chairs were sprinkled about. "Would you like to sit at a table?"

Miranda gracefully planted her seat onto the stool beside his. "This is fine."

Mike sat down again, acutely aware that as he took his seat, his body was captivatingly close to hers. And that the room had become several degrees warmer.

He began to raise his hand to signal the bartender. "What'll you have?" he asked.

Miranda didn't miss a beat. "An apology would be nice."

Mike dropped his hand down again before the bartender looked his way. Turning on his stool, Mike studied the petite, intense woman beside him. It wasn't only the reporter in him that was curious about her, but it made for a good start.

"Your dad an SOS fan?"

Miranda almost laughed then. If ever there was a man devoid of ego, it was her father. He wasn't an easy man to know, keeping everything to himself, but she knew that much. In a world where people were eager to take credit for an accomplishment, her father had always tried to keep out of the limelight. He shunned publicity, both the good and then the bad, wanting only to play the game he loved.

"No, not exactly a fan," she finally acknowledged. If he'd admired his own work—or more importantly, himself—she felt he would have at least attempted to speak up in his own defense rather than stoically accept the commission's ruling that he be barred from baseball. "But he understands the man." As well as anyone could, she added silently.

Her answer only raised more questions. He could see where his article would generate her terse response if her father was a diehard SOS fan and she'd been indoctrinated from the time she was a little girl, but obviously, that wasn't the case.

Mike tried again. "He a gambler, too?"

The smile disappeared and her eyes, an incredible shade of sky-blue, darkened visibly.

"No, he's not."

As a matter of fact, except for that one incident that had brought him down, as far as she knew, her father never gambled. The one time she'd asked him about the details of the incident, he'd watched her for a long moment, then told her to leave it alone. She'd done as he'd asked, but that didn't keep her from wondering.

Mike felt as if he was trying to find his way through an elaborate maze in the dark. "So you just decided to champion Shaw on your own." He leaned forward, creating an intimate space for the two of them. "If you don't mind my asking, why?"

That was why she was here, she reminded herself. "Because Steven Shaw doesn't deserve to be remembered for one isolated moment of weakness, not when he had such an outstanding career from start to finish."

She had a point, but that didn't change the way things were. "Human nature," he told her philosophically. "People tend to remember the bad rather than the good. Especially when they feel they've been betrayed."

Miranda raised her chin defensively. He liked the way fire came into her eyes. "He didn't betray anyone," she protested.

Now, there she was wrong. "His fans felt differently. They believed in him."

"And one transgression changes all that? What kind of fickle fans are they?" she demanded, passion growing in her voice. "For God's sake, he didn't kill anyone. He placed a stupid bet."

Other men could place bets, but not a baseball player. She ought to understand that. "The man broke a cardinal rule."

"I don't remember 'Thou shalt not bet' being one of the Ten Commandments."

"It is in baseball," he pointed out. "If you're a player."

"And God forgives—but the baseball commissioner doesn't, is that it?" she asked sarcastically. On the way over here, she'd promised herself that she'd keep her temper, but she'd had all these feelings bottled up inside for so long. It seemed to her that no one, *no one* had taken her father's side in this.

"Something like that," Mike answered. "If you don't mind my saying so, you don't look like the type to be a baseball groupie."

She'd always hated that term, hated the connotation associated with it: mindless people who blindly followed a team or a player. There was far more to being a true fan of the game than that.

"I'm not," she retorted. "I just love the game. And, I hate injustice."

"So you think that Shaw got a raw deal."

"I *know* he got a raw deal. The man played his heart out at every game. Nothing, but nothing came before baseball for him. The so-called 'offense' took place over ten years ago. The statute of limitations runs out in seven years for everything but murder. Don't you think it's only fair that it run out here, too?"

Maybe, if SOS had had this woman pleading his case, the commission might have been swayed, he mused. She certainly was passionate enough about her cause. "Like I said, baseball has different rules."

Miranda shook her head. "Baseball is the all-American game and America stands for justice, or so we like to think."

"Why are you so adamant about Shaw?" he asked. "From what I hear, the man's almost a recluse."

"He was," she corrected. A hint of pride came into her voice. "Right after the car accident."

It had been touch-and-go for a while. Her father had even been in a coma and some thought he'd never recover. But he did, or at least his body had. But even that was not entirely true. In the last ten years, five operations were needed to make him whole again. Fixing his spirit, however, took even more effort.

"But he's set to start coaching a Little League team now and he's finally coming out of his shell."

Mike thought of all his failed attempts at getting an interview. The woman had really aroused his interest now. Maybe this would be the key to getting to the man. "Sounds as if you know a lot about him."

For a moment, Miranda debated shrugging off his assumption, but that would be lying. And it would seem as if she was ashamed of being Shaw's daughter and she wasn't. She believed in her father, she always had. She was proud to be his daughter, proud of what the man had accomplished. His being banned from baseball didn't change that. Just made her that much more protective of him.

More than anything in the world, she wanted to get her father inducted into the hall of fame. He'd earned the honor. He deserved it.

This sportswriter still waited for an answer. "I make it my business to," she told him.

She saw interest flare in Mike Marlowe's deep blue eyes.

Miranda didn't often act on impulse. Something told her that she'd made a mistake coming here.

Chapter Three

"Do you know SOS personally?"

As he asked the question, Mike could feel his pulse accelerating. He tried to talk himself down. It was too much to hope for, stumbling across a private in with Shaw.

He caught himself hoping anyway. In all ways but one—maintaining lasting relationships—Mike thought of himself as an optimistic guy. And this whimsical meeting might just be the opportunity of his young career.

He glanced at the woman on the bar stool next to his and waited for an answer. He was more than a little convinced that she would affirm his hunch.

Miranda blew out a breath. No doubt about it, this was a mistake. She should have never agreed to this meeting, never mind that she had been the one to suggest it in the heat of the moment. It was a mistake, pure and simple.

Served her right for letting her emotions get the better of her. In that respect, she'd taken after her mother, not her father. Being stoic, like SOS, was simply not in her nature.

Although, God knew she tried. But any good intentions had died the second she'd read Marlowe's column. Someone had to speak up for her father. And look where that had gotten her. Tap dancing madly around words in a sports bar, edging away from an overly eager, overly handsome sportswriter.

Time to retreat.

Miranda slid off the bar stool and slipped her purse strap onto her shoulder. "I have to go," she told him with finality.

Mike read between the lines. Her evasive action told him what he wanted to know. God, but he was glad he'd answered her e-mail. "You *do* know him personally, don't you?"

She hated lying, but she also understood the kind of floodgates that could be opened if she admitted knowing SOS, much less that the former pitcher was her father. She'd been through this more than once.

Still, the word *No* refused to form on her lips this time.

"And if I do?" Miranda hedged.

The excitement built within him. "Then I'd fall to my knees right here and start to beg."

That wasn't what she was expecting him to say.

Amused, she asked, "That might be interesting, but why would you go to such lengths?"

He felt not unlike Aladdin holding the magic lamp in his hands, about to come in contact with the genie for the first time. "For you to use your influence with SOS so that I could land an interview with him."

She knew without having to ask that no way in hell would her father go along with an interview. It had taken her a long time to get the man to communicate with her beyond a few precise words at a time. He wasn't the kind of man to talk to strangers, much less bare his soul to a journalist. Her father was, at bottom, a very private, very shy man. He always had been. She couldn't remember his ever having given an interview. Certainly not since Ariel's death.

And with each devastating incident that occurred in his life—Ariel's death, his divorce, her mother's passing, the scandal and finally, the car accident—her father had just grown more reticent and distant. Even in the best of times, he wasn't someone who liked listening to the sound of his own voice. He preferred doing to talking.

Looking at Mike, she shook her head. "I'm afraid you're out of luck there—"

"On my own, yes," he agreed, talking quickly, "but I've never met anyone who actually had access to the man before."

Miranda had learned how to bob and weave with the best of them. "I didn't say I did," she reminded him.

"You didn't say you didn't."

Fair enough, she thought. He had her there. But she

could remedy that. It meant a small white lie about knowing her father. "Okay, I don't know him."

Mike smiled broadly. "Too late, Miranda. I don't believe you."

Her stomach tightened when he said her name, and she didn't like it. She really needed to get going.

Miranda shook her head. "That has no bearing on the situation."

As she began to leave, Mike stunned her by doing exactly as he'd proposed. He fell to his knees right in front of her, impeding her exit. He caught hold of her wrist—preventing her from just walking around him to the front door.

"Please." The entreaty seemed to vibrate from every pore of his body.

She was acutely aware that people were watching them. Her father's daughter when it came to drawing undue attention, she felt uncomfortable as the center attraction.

"Get up," she blurted, trying unsuccessfully to disengage herself. "People are going to think you're proposing."

He'd rattled her, Mike thought. Good. Maybe he'd get her to see things his way after all. "If that's what it takes to get an interview with SOS…" Mike's voice trailed off.

Her eyes widened. Just her luck to champion her father's cause with a man who was mentally deranged. "You're crazy. You realize that, don't you?"

Mike rose to his feet, still holding on to her wrist. "Look, I've tried to get an interview with SOS half a dozen times—if not more—and he won't return any of my calls."

She could well believe that. Not wanting confrontations or to get into a discussion as to why he wouldn't do an interview, her father would simply just ignore the call altogether.

"He likes to keep to himself," she told him.

"But he's obviously opened up to you." And where Shaw could do it once, Mike was positive the pitcher could do it again.

"I wouldn't call it that." And technically, she was telling the truth. Getting information out of her father— *any* kind of information—took a great deal of time, as well as patience.

Again, Mike saw it for what it was. He prided himself on being able to read people, a combination of body language and attitude. "Look, I get it. You're trying to protect the man. That's really commendable of you. But you also feel that Shaw's gotten a raw deal—"

"He has," she interjected. Then she looked down at her wrist, still caught in his grip. "Am I getting my hand back anytime soon?"

"That depends," he answered.

"On what?"

"On whether you bolt and run the second I let go of it."

Her eyes narrowed. She didn't appreciate these kinds of games, but it was her own fault she was here in the first place. Marlowe certainly hadn't sought her out, she'd come gunning for him.

"I won't 'bolt and run,'" she promised.

Slowly, he spread his fingers out from around her wrist, his eyes remaining on hers. When she continued to remain where she was, he went on.

"Okay, let's say I'm willing to reexamine my position in print. You have to admit that I'd need to talk to the man to do that—which means an interview." He looked at her pointedly. "Can you get me one?"

"And if I did—not saying that I can," she qualified quickly, "how do I know you won't use that to do a hatchet job on him?"

Part of Mike took offense, but he knew where she was coming from. From time to time, Shaw's past transgression drew articles and speculation out of the woodwork. So, he decided to keep his defense simple. "You've read my columns?"

She'd read him faithfully for the last few years, ever since he began to write the column. But to say so might make him feel he had the advantage. "Yes."

"Anything there—before the article on SOS—to make you think that I'm biased or that I have some kind of an ax to grind? Or that I'm laboring under some preset agenda that I've set up for myself?"

She blew out a breath, then shook her head. His columns had always been fair. "No."

Miranda didn't sound a hundred percent convinced. "Ask around if you want to. Anyone in the business'll tell you that I call it the way I see it and I'm nobody's lackey." He'd laid his cards on the table and he held his breath. "Now, do I get an interview with the man?"

Even if she wanted him to have it, she couldn't

make that kind of promise. "That's not up to me, that's up to him."

"So you do have some influence."

She'd walked right into that one, hadn't she? Miranda upbraided herself. Another mistake. But, try as she might, she couldn't work up any anger against the sportswriter. "I wouldn't exactly say that."

"What are you, his assistant?"

The time for denying that she knew her father was obviously over. Inclining her head, she gave him a non-answer. "I'm whatever he needs me to be."

The simply stated affirmation stopped Mike in his tracks for a second. What she said could be interpreted in a number of ways, some of which he found himself not exactly happy about. If she was saying what he thought she was saying, that made her out of bounds. If she was romantically involved with the former major-league pitcher, he wasn't about to act on any of the impulses he's been entertaining for the last few minutes.

In his opinion, Miranda whatever-her-last-name-was was far too young for Shaw, but then, this day and age, anything was possible. Besides, it really wasn't any of his business.

"I see." Mike focused on what *was* important. "So, you'll ask him?"

"Do you promise if you do get to talk to him, you'll write a fair article?"

"I promise." Like a boy taking an oath, Mike swiped his index finger across his heart, making an X. An amused smile played on his lips. "Cross my heart and hope to die."

In contrast, Miranda's smile was sharp and devoid of humor. "You lie to me, and you will."

This Shaw had to really be something else in private to arouse that kind of loyalty. He was going to get an interview, he thought, hardly able to believe his luck.

"So when can I meet him?"

"You're getting ahead of yourself," she pointed out. "I didn't say I'd ask him—and even if I do ask him, there's probably a very good chance that he'll say no. He doesn't like reporters," she explained honestly. Reporters were like vultures, he'd once told her, except that they didn't wait until the victim was dead before they started stripping off the flesh.

"I'm a journalist," Mike corrected.

How was that different? "A rose by any other name…" Miranda let her voice trail off as she eyed him pointedly.

He needed leverage. Mike decided to share something with her.

"Would it further my case for you to know that when I was a kid, SOS was my hero? That I can remember exactly where I was and what I was doing the day I heard about the betting scandal and that he'd been banned from baseball for life?" He paused for a second, debating, then added, "I cried myself to sleep that night. Not even my brothers know that."

Yes, it helped, she thought. If what he said was true. If so, then he'd be more likely to *want* to find a way to get the public to come around. And wasn't this what she'd wanted all along, someone to champion her father's case in print? Who better than an established sportswriter who'd once been a devoted fan?

Slowly, she nodded in response to his question. "I'm sorry you lost your hero."

"Yeah, me, too. Who knows, maybe I'll find him again." If SOS told him why he'd placed the bets when he knew it went against the rules, maybe it would finally make sense to him. Mike tried to contain his eagerness—after all, nothing had been cast in stone yet. For all he knew, the woman might be pulling his leg. "So you'll talk to him about giving me an interview?"

"I'll see what I can do."

"Great. Terrific."

Damn, but he almost felt like a kid again, experiencing that exhilarating rush when he got to go to a ball game on picture day and was able to collect autographs of his favorite players. Kate always made sure he was in the front row when the players came out, maneuvering her way through the crowd and bringing him with her.

He felt like celebrating. "Sure I can't buy you a drink?"

She shook her head. "I'm sure." She'd suggested the sports bar because it was close, not because she liked beer. Her preference ran toward drinks that came with tiny colorful parasols—but she was driving and she didn't have the time to spare, waiting for the drink to dissipate into her bloodstream. "I've got to be going," she reminded him.

"Right. Oh, wait." He'd gotten so excited, he'd almost forgotten the most important part. "How do I get in contact with you?"

He obviously wasn't thinking because otherwise,

Miranda decided, he would have remembered the e-mail. But because she didn't want to embarrass him, she didn't bother pointing that out.

"I'll get in contact with you," she replied. She liked it better that way. It put the ball in her court and gave her control. Control was important to her. So very little of life came under that heading. "Do you have a business card?"

"Yeah, sure." Mike immediately felt for his wallet.

Once retrieved from his left rear pocket, he flipped it open. Aside from several torn bits of paper containing miscellaneous information, two credit cards, several twenties, his driver's license, a press card and a photograph of his family taken at the last fourth of July celebration, there was nothing. He'd forgotten to replenish his supply of business cards.

"Just not with me," he muttered, then looked up. "Sorry, I gave away my last one a few days ago," he apologized. Pulling a napkin over from the bar, he took out a pen and began to write down every phone number he could think of where she could reach him. "This is my cell number, my office number and my landline at home." He pointed to each. "Call me anytime, night or day."

She took the napkin from him and folded it into her purse. Her attention was drawn to the photograph he'd shuffled through in his search for the business card.

"Is that your family?" They appeared to be a happy bunch of people, she thought, wondering what it felt like to have a large family. Now there was only her father and her.

"What?" His mind already on the interview he wanted to conduct, it took Mike a second to process her question. "Oh, yes, that's my family. My brothers, my sister, my dad and my stepmother."

Taking the photograph from him, she got a closer look. "My God, your brothers are absolutely identical," she said in awe. Initially, when she'd glanced at the photograph, she'd thought her eyes were playing tricks on her.

"Not once you get to know them," Mike assured her. Growing up, Mike had gotten so used to his brothers he hadn't thought of them as triplets in years. He put the photograph back into his wallet, which he tucked into his pocket. "How about you?"

Miranda looked at him, slightly confused. "How about me what?"

"Do you have a business card?"

She did. It had her name, her position and Promise Pharmaceuticals' very ornate logo stamped across it. But she didn't really want Mike Marlowe having that much information on her, especially not her last name. She wanted to be the one who called the shots and could quietly disappear in case her father couldn't be convinced to do this interview.

The more she thought about it, the more certain she was that Marlowe could redeem her father. The only way people were going to change their minds about him was if someone methodically—and passionately—laid out all the arguments to let the past go and reevaluate the man only in terms of his accomplishments.

She shook her head, spreading her hands wide. "I'm afraid I don't have a card with me."

Mike leaned over the bar and confiscated another napkin. Pulling it over, he held it out to her along with his pen. "That's okay." He grinned. "We can exchange napkins."

She placed her hand over his and lightly pushed it back down to the bar. "I'd really rather just keep it this way if you don't mind."

He raised one eyebrow. "In other words, don't call us, we'll call you?" he asked.

"Not exactly. Something a little less daunting than that," she promised, squaring her shoulders. There was something very sexy about a woman who knew her own mind. Damn, but that Shaw was a lucky man, he thought. "I'll be in touch."

"I'll hold you to that," Mike called after her.

Miranda didn't turn around, but she did lift her hand above her head, giving him a half wave of acknowledgment.

Mike squelched the urge to sprint in order to walk out the door with the woman. He had a feeling she might equate that to come kind of a power play and he didn't want anything jeopardizing the interview. So instead, he leaned back against his stool and watched her exit…and the way her hips subtly moved to some beat only she heard. The number of patrons at the bar had increased considerably since he'd arrived, Mike couldn't help thinking.

Just as she disappeared through the door, whatever else might have comprised Shaw's shortcomings, the man certainly knew how to pick his women.

Chapter Four

"Son of a—gun."

Glancing toward his left, Mike amended his language out of deference to his stepmother, in whose kitchen he was sitting. Twenty years ago, she had come into his life bearing puppets, warm humor and good intentions. She'd wound up staying on to raise him and his brothers, not as their nanny the way she'd initially appeared, but as their new mother. Along the way, she'd also accomplished the impossible by making his dad smile again.

There'd been a very dark period, right after his mother died in that plane crash. He was five and his brothers were four; they'd been utterly certain none of them would ever be all right again. To this day, the sharp, biting pain of that loss, of suddenly realizing that his mother would never return, never walk through the front door and hug him again, remained with him, hovering in the shadows.

But that took nothing away from Kate. Blond, chipper and incredibly intuitive when it came to the actions of small boys, she had brought light into their world and subsequently turned them into a family again. Though words were his craft, he could never really tell Kate the full extent of how much she had come to mean to him. To all of them.

Kate was sensitive to cursing, so he stopped himself before he uttered anything offensive. But had he shouted out "Rumplestiltskin," that still wouldn't have taken the edge off his surprise.

Mike stared at the screen and the article he'd just pulled up after Googling Steven Shaw's personal stats. Mike wasn't sure what to think and part of him felt like an idiot.

"Something wrong?" Kate asked, her voice an equal mixture of amusement and concern.

She peered over her shoulder, away from the stove and the dinner she was preparing. It wasn't a throw-away, automatic question. Kate was interested in every aspect of her sons' lives and was more than willing to listen to anything they felt like sharing. The little boys that she'd once signed on to raise were off on their own now. Nothing made her happier than having them all turn up around the table at the same time for a meal. She asked for one day a month. Generous, they tried to give her one day a week whenever they could coordinate their schedules. It meant the world to her.

The others, including her husband, weren't here yet, but Mike had decided to come over early, with the one stipulation that he be allowed to bring his work with him because he needed to get something done before this evening. Kate was so pleased to have him come over—he'd missed the last couple of get-togethers because he was out of town on assignment—she would have said yes if he'd asked to bring the devil along.

There was a five-second delay before her question played itself in his brain.

"What?" He looked up, then shook his head. "Oh, no, nothing's wrong." He glanced back at the screen and the startling information. "Exactly," he amended.

Kate dug a little deeper. "Would you like to elaborate on that just a little?"

Mike frowned, still looking at the screen. "I think she's his daughter."

"'His'?" she prodded.

"Shaw. Steven Orin Shaw." He addressed her. "I think someone I spoke to a couple of days ago was Shaw's daughter. I didn't know he had more than one—the one who died," he filled in, not expecting his stepmother to remember. "But it says right here that he had two, Ariel and Miranda."

Kate watched him with mild interest. "You know a Miranda?"

"I don't really know her, I just met her," he qualified. "She sent me an angry e-mail—"

Kate laughed. "I can hear the wedding bells ringing already."

"Sorry to disappoint you, but it's not like that, Kate," he said, shaking his head.

"You could never disappoint me, Mike," she told him matter-of-factly. "And neither could your brothers or Kelsey."

Maybe not, but he and the guys knew that their stepmother had her heart set on getting them married and having babies of their own. She would have liked nothing better than to have the house crammed with the sounds of growing families. And while that might happen down the road for his brothers and little sister, he doubted it would happen for him.

For one thing, he wasn't looking to get married. The odds were just too great that he'd be signing on for major disappointment down the line. He could still remember how his father looked when he received the news of the plane crash. How devastated he was. There was no way he would ever willingly set himself up for that kind of heartache. And, with attachment came the very real possibility of heartache.

"This has to do with work," he told her. "I wrote a piece about why Steven Shaw shouldn't be considered a viable candidate for induction into the baseball hall of fame, and she wrote in to comment."

Kate nodded. "Right, Shaw," she said. "The pitcher who disappointed you so badly."

"You actually remember that?" Mike stared at his stepmother in surprise.

Kate turned away from the stove and the potatoes she was mashing. She set down the container of parmesan cheese after sprinkling some into the mixture.

"Why do you sound so surprised? I remember everything about you boys." Sympathy entered her eyes. "I remember how upset you were when you found out that Shaw was banned from baseball. That was the year you wanted to throw away all your sports memorabilia."

Memories he hadn't thought about in a long time returned to him. "You stopped me from tearing up his autograph."

She'd rescued the photograph just in time. He'd pulled it free of its frame and was just about to destroy it when she walked into the room. "I thought that you might regret it later, when you stopped being so angry at him."

"I would have," he admitted, because it represented a piece of his past, not because it belonged to Shaw. "I never did say thanks."

Kate shrugged. "Being family means you don't have to say it—but I admit that once in a while, it is nice to hear." Picking up the container of cheese, she got back to work. "So, who's this Miranda person who sent you that e-mail?"

"Apparently, his daughter." He thought about the woman again. Why would she have kept that a secret? It didn't make sense to him and he hated things that didn't make sense. "I mean, her name's Miranda and it says here that Shaw's got a daughter named Miranda. It's not exactly on the list of the most popular names of the past decade. How many Mirandas are there out there?"

Chuckling, she wiped her hands on a towel. "Afraid I haven't taken a survey on that lately, but my guess is not too many." Kate crossed to him and draped her arm over his shoulder. He had a Web page opened to the former pitcher's biography. "Is that good or bad—that she's his daughter, I mean."

"Good—if she can get that interview for me." However, his optimism regarding his chances was dwindling. "But I haven't heard from her in a couple of days."

"Call her."

Mike shook his head. "Can't."

"What's stopping you?"

He looked a tad sheepish, "I don't have her number."

"That would do it." Kate paused for a second, thinking. In this day and age of the information highway, nothing stayed hidden for long. "Seems to me that a man with your connections should be able to locate the daughter of one of the all-time great pitchers of our time."

He grinned. He knew a couple of people to contact, one of whom was all but hardwired to his computer. "I'll do it after the Super Bowl."

The Super Bowl. Kate stifled a sigh. She didn't want Mike seeing her disappointment. "That's right, you're flying out to cover the game. Lucky you." And then, she added, "We'll miss you at the party."

He had to be honest. He'd almost prefer to stay for the family get-together than fly down to the game in Florida. The Super Bowl party had been a major deal around the Marlowe household for the last twenty years.

It still amazed him how Kate had managed to take

his father—who'd had no interest in sports—and get him involved in events that celebrated the pinnacle of each sport just because he and his brothers were into it. Kate was a firm believer in family solidarity.

Just then, Travis entered the kitchen. He paused to kiss Kate on the cheek and nod at his older brother. It was obvious that he'd overheard the last part of the conversation.

"Right, we'll all be crying into our pizza for poor Mikey, who's forced to sit there in the press box, watching the Packers play the Chargers up close and personal." His sarcastic tone turned wistful. "I'd give my eyeteeth to be there." Opening the refrigerator, Travis took out a bottle of beer and twisted off the cap. He closed the door, leaned against it and took a sip. "Now, if either Trent or Trevor had been the sportswriter, I could tie him up, leave him in his apartment and then go in his place. Nobody would be the wiser."

"Until you started to write the article and they found out that you were illiterate." Mike grinned and scrutinized the oldest of the triplets. "Been giving this setup a lot of thought, have you?"

"A ton," Travis admitted solemnly. "And I'm green with envy."

"We'll have a good time here," Kate promised Travis. "Now, go set the table for me."

Travis set his beer down on the counter and pretended to protest. "Mike was here first, how come you didn't tell him to set the table?"

"Because I'm doing research," Mike answered, pointing to the laptop.

"He's pulling your leg, you know," Travis told Kate as he crossed to the cupboard. "He's probably just surfing the Net for sports memorabilia."

"Be that as it may—" Kate retired the serving spoon she was using and paused to pat Travis's face "—you're neater."

"I am that," Travis readily agreed. Opening the cupboard, he took down seven dinner plates.

"You missed your calling, you know," Mike told his stepmother as his brother went into the dining room with the plates. "Instead of a child psychologist, you should have become part of the diplomatic corps. They could have used someone like you."

"Smoothing out the waves in this family is all the challenge I need or want," Kate assured her husband's firstborn with a warm smile. She couldn't have loved him and his brothers any more if they'd been hers from the moment they'd drawn breath.

Shutting down his computer, Mike snapped the laptop lid closed and rose from the counter. "I'll go help Travis so he'll stop griping."

She flashed another smile. "Knew I could count on you."

Miranda made her way across the neatly trimmed grass, doing her best to place most of her weight on her toes. Her heels insisted on sinking into the soft soil if she paused. The terrain was not high-heel friendly, but she hadn't had the time to go home to change.

She'd come here straight from work, surprising Tilda because ordinarily she stayed one or two hours after quitting time if she got involved in what she was doing—which was most of the time. She loved her work, loved the idea of being involved in something that could help people, possibly cure them or at least alleviate their pains.

The only thing she loved more was her father.

"Leaving on time twice in one week," Tilda had said as she gathered together her own things. "People are going to start saying you actually have a life away from here."

Miranda made sure that her machine shut down. Lately, it had a tendency to go into sleep mode instead.

"Today's my dad's first day as coach for that Little League team." It was the end of January, but things began earlier these days. Seasons that once began in March now started in January, allowing more practice games. In this case that was a good thing. She wanted her father busy and involved in something other than the pain of the past.

"And you want to make sure he shows up."

Miranda hated to admit it, but her friend was right. However, she had shrugged evasively. "Something like that."

She'd driven all the way here from the lab, praying she and the kids who turned up tonight wouldn't be disappointed.

When she'd parked in the lot of Greenwood Elementary School, Miranda scanned the area for her father's big black van. He insisted on driving himself around rather than allowing his assistant, a former linebacker named Walter, to chauffeur him around. Driving afforded him a certain kind of independence he refused to surrender. The van had been customized to accommodate his special needs. More than that, it gave him back a portion of his dignity. She knew the way her father thought. A man who could drive himself around was in charge of his own destiny, at least to some extent. A man who was driven around was not.

The fateful car accident had initially robbed him not just of his mobility, but of all feeling from the neck on down. Slowly, miraculously, several operations gave him back some of that feeling *and* mobility, returning it by inches. But even before the operations had begun, she had insisted that Steven Orin Shaw was more than the sum of his parts, repeating it over and over again like an ancient mantra. By the time he had finally been discharged from the rehab facility, she'd managed to burrow through the wall he'd built up around himself and awaken his pride, which in turn caused his iron resolve to kick in again.

Without that, he would have been a goner before the first month was out. Instead, he began not only to function but also to thrive—in his own way.

This was the best thing for him, she thought, coming up to the fenced-off area where a small group of nine- and ten-year-old boys and girls sat restlessly, their stored-up energy all but bursting. As was the custom, the children wore uniforms. At the beginning of a new season, each group of children got to adopt an actual major league team. Part of the process meant dressing like that team for the duration of the season.

Her father's coaching career began with the Cubs. He'd never been that crazy about the actual Cubs, having been initially passed over by their minor league counterparts at the very beginning of his career. But it was a start, she thought, mentally crossing her fingers as she approached him.

"Hi, how's it going?" she called out.

Putting down his roster, Steve Shaw frowned in response. He turned the wheelchair around to face her directly. For two cents, he'd aim his chair at the parking lot and just keep going.

"It's not. I don't know anything about coaching kids," he grumbled, barely lowering his voice to keep it from carrying to the kids assembled behind him. He gazed up into his daughter's eyes. He knew she meant well, but the road to hell was paved with good intentions and this would have qualified as one of them. "This was a bad idea, Randy."

At least he was using the nickname he'd given her instead of her formal name. She took heart in that. "It's a good idea, Dad," she countered, undaunted. "Remember, the whole idea behind this is for all of you to have fun, nothing more."

That was far too P.C. for him. He'd never been one of those people for whom winning was everything, however, it was a large part of who he was—or at least who he had once been. "And to win," he added.

"That's part of the fun," she told him, flashing a large, sunny smile she hoped was contagious. She patted her father's shoulder, aware that at least fifteen sets of eyes observed every movement. She lowered her voice and leaned in. "You can do this, Dad. You're a natural."

"And you're a con artist, Randy."

Miranda spread her hands. "I'm whatever I have to be." Her answer reminded her of the promise she'd made to Marlowe. She'd said almost the same thing to the sportswriter when he'd asked if she was SOS's assistant. Her timing was probably off, but she needed to do it now, before her courage failed her. "Dad?"

Steven raised his eyes to his daughter's face. "Yeah?"

"There's this sportswriter—" Her father's expression instantly became almost dour. Only dogged determination made her continue. When she was younger, that look would have had her lapsing into silence or even backing out of the room. But she wasn't a little girl anymore. "He'd like to interview you."

"No." The tone left no room for argument.

"Dad, it might not be such a bad thing. He said you were his idol."

Shaw snorted dismissively. "They say anything to get to you. Flattery, lies, doesn't matter. All that matters is getting an interview—and then turning it into whatever they want."

She thought of the man she'd talked to in the bar. God help her, she might be wrong, but she added, "I believe him, Dad."

Steven waved away the notion. "Then you do the interview."

"Dad—"

Turning his wheelchair abruptly away, he gave her his back. "Case closed, Randy. Now, if you really want me to do this—" he waved his hand at the kids who were watching them "—I need to concentrate."

One battle at a time, she told herself. "I really want you to do this," she assured him, surrendering—for the time being.

"Then call them over for me and let's get explaining the rules over with."

"You get to have some of the dads as assistant coaches," she reminded him.

The reminder brought no joy to him. Steven shook his head. In his experience, too many coaches fouled things up and created more problems. "This just keeps getting better and better," he murmured.

"Yes," she told him, squeezing his hand, "it does." Crossing back to the fenced-in area, she motioned to the children. "C'mon over here, kids. The coach wants to talk to you."

A handful of fathers and mothers had opted to hang around rather than just to drop off their offspring and return for them.

A tall, lanky man in jeans and a fisherman's sweater hurriedly crossed over to her.

"Hi, I'm Jake Marshall, Billy's father." He pointed over to the group. "Is that really—" He lowered his voice. "Steve Shaw? SOS," he added, just in case she was uninformed.

"Yes," she told him, trying to gauge the man's intentions. To her relief, he beamed like a small boy.

"Wow. Never thought my kid would be coached by a living legend like SOS."

She smiled back. The man's reaction made up her mind for her. She was going to call Marlowe the moment she got home. Her father *needed* to give this interview.

Chapter Five

That night, after the game was over, Miranda stopped for a while at her father's house just to celebrate his surviving his first day as a Little League coach. It was hard to tell how he felt about the whole thing because he rarely displayed any sort of emotion, but he seemed ever so slightly pleased with the outcome of the session. It was something to build on.

When she finally got home, she called Mike. She got his voice mail, so she left a message saying she wanted to talk about doing the interview.

She assumed that would be enough to get the sportswriter to call the second he checked his messages. But when twenty-four hours had passed, she began to worry that perhaps he'd changed his mind about doing the interview. Granted, it had been his suggestion, but the more she thought about it, the more she warmed up to the idea.

Not that her father was going to cooperate, at least not right away. Her idea was to have the sportswriter observe her father coaching the kids. She was fairly confident the man would have a good start. If he engaged her father in a conversation, there was no reason for her father to know that Mike was a reporter if he didn't identify himself. By the time the first coaching session had come to a close, a great many of the players' fathers had shown up, all drawn to the field in order to see the great Steve Orin Shaw up close and personal. If he played his cards right, Marlowe could just be part of the crowd.

Her father was a man of few words, but he wasn't rude if someone spoke to him. Once he did speak, Marlowe would see just what kind of a person her father was: a decent man who didn't deserve what had happened to him no matter what the rules said.

Miranda tried calling Mike again.

And again.

And again.

"Damn," she muttered under her breath, snapping the flip phone closed and terminating her latest attempt to get through. By now it was late Friday afternoon and she'd tried all the numbers Marlowe had scribbled on the napkin. She'd gotten voice mail on his cell phone, on his office extension and the landline number she assumed was his home. Frustration made her antsy.

The uncustomary glimpse of temper had Tilda looking in her direction. Her best friend didn't bother to hide her amusement. "You know, for an even-tempered person, you seem pretty agitated these last few days. Other than a full moon, what's up?"

"That sportswriter I met with the other day, Mike Marlowe, the one who wanted to interview my father…" she said by way of a reminder in case Tilda had forgotten. "Well, I decided that maybe doing the interview would be a good thing after all." She looked accusingly at the cell phone in her hand before she returned it to her pocket. "And now I can't reach him."

Tilda seemed mildly interested. "You sure you're calling the right number?"

"Oh, I'm sure." The numbers on the napkin were surprisingly legible. "I keep getting his voice mail."

"Don't you know what this weekend is?" When Miranda eyed her blankly, Tilda laughed. "It's Super Bowl Sunday—the most holy of holy days for football fanatics…and sportswriters, I imagine. Your sportswriter isn't snubbing you, he's probably working."

"He's not my sportswriter," Miranda corrected. "He's just a means to an end."

"Either way," Tilda said, returning to her experiment, "you're just going to have to curb your impatience until Monday."

Miranda sighed. Tilda was right. But now that she'd made up her mind, waiting until Monday wasn't going to be easy.

The ringing noise slowly registered as she got ready for work. It wasn't exactly the crack of dawn but it wasn't a normal hour for anyone to be calling her. Still sleepy, her first response was to automatically grab the telephone receiver next to her bed. She found herself mumbling, "Hello? Hello?" to a dial tone. The ringing persisted. It wasn't coming from the phone.

The door.

Someone was at the door.

Her thoughts instantly flew to her father. Someone was at the door because something had happened to her father. It had to be Walter, the man she'd insisted on hiring to stay with her father to help him with all the small tasks that everyone took for granted until they couldn't do them.

She could feel her chest constrict. Trying to brace herself for the worst, Miranda made her way to the door. She turned lights on all the way, to buoy her spirits a little.

But when she looked through the peephole, she didn't see the six-foot-five, 245-pound former linebacker on the other side. She saw the sportswriter she'd been trying to reach.

He was here now?

What the hell was wrong with him? Didn't he know normal people left for work at this time?

And how did he get her address?

Maybe her eyes were playing tricks on her. "Who *is* it?"

His answer eliminated any doubt about her eyesight. "It's Mike Marlowe," he said. "I just got in."

With a sigh, Miranda flipped back both locks on her front door and then pulled it open. She stood on the doorway, blocking his access. "From where? London?"

"The east coast. Florida." He tried not to stare, but her suit framed her body, accentuating the length of her bare legs. And highlighting the body in between. "I just got your message," he told her, trying not to sound as eager as he felt.

Miranda let out a long breath. She hadn't gotten all that that much sleep, having put in a long evening with her father. He was doing poorly again, although he didn't want to admit it. He hated owning up to feeling any sort of pain, but she knew the signs. He'd been through five operations since the accident in an attempt to continue correcting the damage he'd sustained in the collision that had very nearly ended his life.

The orthopedic surgeon had warned her from the beginning that her father was going to be faced with at least eight to ten operations before it was all over. Perhaps more. The prospect was emotionally draining. So she was trying to stay optimistic and positive for both their sakes.

She stepped back, allowing Mike to enter. "And you couldn't wait until later this morning to call back?"

"Oh. Sorry." He flashed her a boyish grin as he came in. If she wasn't so tired, she would have found it charming. "I'm still on east coast time," he apologized.

"How nice for you," she mumbled. She rubbed the back of her neck. Now that she knew there was no emergency, she'd sunk back into exhaustion again. "Look, can you come back later? When I'm not in a rush to get to work?"

"Yeah, sure." He took a step back toward the door, then stopped. "But you are serious?" he couldn't help asking. "You're not just trying to jerk me around for some reason?"

"About seeing you later?" she guessed. "Yes, I'm serious."

"No," he contradicted impatiently, "about what you said in your message. That I can actually interview your father."

Okay, she was awake again. She was damn sure she hadn't said anything about SOS being her father.

Miranda shut the door and looked at him. "How did you find out Steve Shaw was my father?"

"I did a little digging," he told her simply. "I found out that SOS has a second daughter named Miranda."

A second daughter. That was the way she'd always felt. The second daughter. The spare that came after Ariel. Banking down her thoughts, Miranda pressed her lips together and shrugged. "That could be just a coincidence."

"Could be," he allowed, his eyes meeting hers, "but it isn't."

"And my address? How did you get that?" She was unlisted, so he couldn't have gotten it from the phonebook or any listing online.

"I called in a few favors," he admitted. As he spoke, he studied her face to see her reaction. "Even sportswriters have their ways." He became serious. "Why didn't you tell me you were Shaw's daughter?"

"Maybe because I didn't want some overeager sportswriter camping out on my doorstep." The minute the words were out, Miranda felt a twinge of regret. She wasn't usually snippy like this. "Sorry, I'm not at my best in the morning."

"No, it's all my fault," Mike said. "I should have waited until later. I'm afraid that I didn't realize what time it was. I heard your message a minute after I walked into my apartment. I guess I just got too excited about doing the interview to think clearly."

"Yes, about that—"

He heard the hesitation in her voice. "You've changed your mind again?" he asked.

Because if she had, he was going to do his damnedest to talk her back into letting him do the interview. This was the closest he'd come to landing it and he was not about to let the opportunity slip through his fingers without a fight.

Miranda folded her arms in front of her chest. "No, I haven't changed my mind. Well, actually, I have—but in your favor," she was quick to add before he could bury her in rhetoric. "I decided that your doing a piece on my father—the man behind all that negative talk— would probably be a good thing." Her eyes pinned him for a moment. "As long as you do an honest article. Because if you don't," she warned him, still smiling, "I'll hunt you down and cut your heart out."

Looking at her, he would have never guessed her capable of this kind of passion. Just showed that it was true what they said about books and their covers. "You have my word," he told her solemnly.

She shook her head. "I don't know you so your word doesn't mean anything to me."

He never wavered beneath her scrutiny. "It does to me."

She was silent for a moment. Okay, maybe she believed him. "Point taken," she finally said. "But what I was trying to get at is that my father won't do an interview. Not with you, not with anyone—"

Mike refused to give up. "Can't you talk him into it?"

She laughed softly. "No one can talk my father into anything. He doesn't yell or get angry, he will just politely ignore what he doesn't agree with. But just because he won't subject himself to a formal interview," she went on, "doesn't mean you can't talk to him."

Mike cocked his head slightly. "I don't think I follow you."

"It's called conversation." The look on Mike's face just grew more confused. "Let me backtrack—"

"Please."

Miranda couldn't help smiling. Marlowe had a rather pleasant voice and that particular word had a nice, almost alluring ring when he said it.

She realized her mind was wandering and forced herself to focus.

"My father just began coaching a Little League team last week. The faces are still new to him. I thought you might come, mingle in with the fathers and observe him for a little while, see how he interacts with the kids. That way, you can talk to him and he won't suspect that you're actually a sportswriter."

He hadn't expected this. "In other words, you want me to deceive your father."

She decided to put her cards on the table. The man who had tracked her down was sharp enough to figure out the rest without too much effort. She might as well tell him and save them both some time.

"What I want is to have my father inducted into the hall of fame." She saw the protest forming on Mike's lips and quickly went on. "He deserves it and he has a right to be in it. Once you get to know him, you'll agree with me. The only way my father has a ghost of a chance is if there's a grassroots movement among the fans to have him inducted."

"And if I don't agree with you?" he countered.

"You will." Her faith was unshakable.

But Mike was skeptical about what she was proposing. After all, he'd just put forth a whole article against possible induction. "And you want me to plead his case?"

She didn't want him to think she was trying to put something over on him, or asking him to go against his principles. She was convinced that if Mike gave her father a chance, he would be won over. Not by charm, but by decency.

"I want you to do an honest portrayal of the man. The rest," she promised, "will take care of itself." She paused, then drew in a long breath, waiting for his answer. "So, what do you say?"

He laughed softly, shaking his head. "I say you're being wasted in drug research. You have it in you to make a hell of a campaign manager for some fledgling politician."

"Not interested in that," she said, dismissing the notion. "I'm just interested in getting my father what he deserves."

She didn't add that she wanted to do it quickly. She

didn't know how much time her father had left. There were days that his condition worsened and she worried that he might take a nosedive. Not a great believer in omens, she just couldn't shake the feeling of urgency that pervaded her.

With Mike's article appearing just when it did, things just seemed to fall into place.

And then she suddenly did a mental replay. Mike had just said something about the nature of her work. That wasn't just a lucky guess. He knew what she did for a living. Something else she hadn't volunteered.

She looked at him uneasily. "What else do you know about me?"

"Only the basic facts."

He didn't mention that when he'd discovered that she wasn't Shaw's girlfriend or mistress, but was his daughter, a feeling of relief had washed over him. For that he owed his former college roommate, Frank Jessop, one hell of a night out on the town—when he could spare the time. A computer-programming wizard who worked as a consultant for several government intelligence agencies, Jessop could get an erased hard drive to give up its invisible secrets.

Because she appeared to be waiting, Mike explained. "That you graduated at the top of your class at UCLA and that you went into pharmaceutical research because your older sister, Ariel, died of a rare blood disease." He paused for a second before adding, "And that you're not seeing anyone currently."

Her father and her work took up all her free time. Besides, she didn't miss what she had never had and she'd been too busy these last couple of years to have much of a social life beyond occasionally getting together with Tilda after hours for a little girltalk.

"Is that last part important?" she asked. As far as she could see, her life had no bearing on her father's.

It had been to him, Mike thought. "Everything's important in its place," he told her.

Miranda had no idea why a shiver suddenly slipped down her spine. She attributed it to lack of sleep and that her decision to go behind her father's back was not sitting well with her conscience.

She pushed the thoughts away. "Would you like to stay for breakfast?" she asked suddenly.

"Maybe not breakfast." He definitely wasn't hungry at the moment. The dinner he'd had on the flight back was laying like lead on his stomach. "But I can be talked in to coffee."

Amused, she asked, "How much talking would I have to do?"

He pretended to think a minute. "Just say the word *coffee*."

Her mouth curved beguilingly as she played along. "Coffee."

"That'll do it." Mike grinned broadly, enjoying himself. He still couldn't believe he would be in the proximity of Steve Orin Shaw. The disappointed twelve-year-old gave way to the fan that had existed before. And then he thought of the repercussions. He wasn't the kind of reporter for whom the story was all-important above everything else. He wasn't the type to close his eyes to the possible consequences.

"Is this going to get you into trouble with your father?" he asked, following her into the kitchen. "I mean, you know he is going to find out once the article is out. Somebody will tell him about it."

That part was true. Even at his lowest point, when he tried to leave the world behind and live like a hermit, some of his old friends still kept in touch. Even when he didn't answer. They'd tell him about the article in the *Times* and ask if he changed his mind about doing interviews.

"He might stop talking to me for a while, but then, he's not much of a talker anyway so the difference will be negligible."

He watched her take a can of coffee out from the refrigerator and shut the door with a swift nudge of her hip. "What was it like," he asked, "growing up being SOS's daughter?"

She didn't have to think about her answer. "Lonely. My mother, sister and I were stationary," she explained. "Dad was on the road a good deal of the time, either with the team, or doing promotional work or in training camp. Looking back, it seemed as if he was hardly ever home," she admitted. Miranda smiled, more to herself than at Mike. "But whenever he was home, it was just like Christmas. He'd bring us presents and listen to us talk on and on about what we were doing. I don't think I ever heard my father raise his voice. And the only time I ever saw him angry was when Ariel died. He punched a wall right before the funeral. He had to go to the ceremony with his hand all bandaged up." A sad smile played on her lips. "I bandaged it for him because my mother was too upset to do it and he refused to go to the E.R."

The coffee machine began to make noises, announcing its progress. She took down two mugs and set them on the counter.

"I guess that was the beginning of the end, really. My mother blamed my father for Ariel's death, said it was his genes that were responsible. He had a great uncle who died of the same thing. They stopped talking to each other." She drew in a deep breath and then released it. "The divorce wasn't a surprise to anyone but me." And then she looked at him suddenly as she realized what she'd said. "You're not going to put that into the article, are you?"

Integrity trumped a scoop every time. "I'd like to, but I won't if you don't want me to."

Miranda shook her head. "It's not about me, it's about him."

"But you're part of him." The way he saw it, you couldn't have one without the other.

Her smile was rueful. "I'm trying to be," she admitted, "but I don't think my father quite sees it that way." Finished with its brew cycle, the coffee machine fell silent. She picked up the coffeepot and filled first one mug, then the other. She offered the first to him. "Help yourself to sugar." Miranda nodded at the half-filled small crystal bowl on the table. "There's milk in the refrigerator."

"Black is fine," he said, picking up the mug.

As they sipped their coffee, a comfortable stillness softly descended, embracing them both. Miranda held her mug in both hands, silently studying the man in her kitchen.

Mike Marlowe was the right man for the job, she decided. She was doing the right thing.

Chapter Six

Getting out of her car, Miranda took a deep breath and let it out again. She was still a little shaky inside.

"This has to be what spies feel like," she said out loud.

Mike was already waiting for her. From the way he leaned against his two-seater, he'd been there for a while. The amused expression on his face told her that he'd heard her.

Her car keys slipped out of her hands, landing with a semi-melodic clatter on the recently repaved asphalt.

Mike bobbed down and got them before she had a chance to do it herself.

Holding the keys out to her, he smiled. "Not successful ones," he countered whimsically. When she raised an eyebrow quizzically, he explained. "You're nervous."

There was no point in denying it. Ordinarily, she was pretty cool under fire, but this was her father, which changed everything. "I've never gone behind his back before."

She expected Mike to laugh or say something about her reacting like an adolescent. Instead, he seemed to understand.

"I can pretend not to know you," Mike volunteered. "Say I got an anonymous tip that he'd be here—but for all we know, he might not find out who, or rather what—I am."

The so-called "anonymous tip" would be to cover up her part in this. "Then you'd be the one lying."

Mike was completely unfazed, but then, she rather suspected he would be. She wasn't prepared for her own reaction to his answer.

"We like to call it poetic license," he told her, punctuating his words with a wink that went straight to her gut. It fluttered and quivered before tightening again.

Miranda paused for a second and actually debated his cover story, but then she noticed her father glancing in their direction. "Too late," she murmured, "he sees me talking to you."

"Just a stranger to the area checking to make sure he's in the right place," Mike supplied without a moment's hesitation.

Obviously "poetic license" came easily to him, she thought.

Looking to the center of the field and the batting cage, Mike frowned slightly. "That's a hell of a long distance for your father to be able to see anything." He could barely make out the man's expression, which appeared dour—but that could just be his eyes playing tricks on him.

"My father's always had fantastic vision," she told him. "Even now."

Just went along with the mystique, Mike thought. Everything about the man seemed a little larger than life. Even his accident lent itself to that. According to the news media, SOS should have died instantly at the scene. And when he hadn't, the doctors all said he would be completely paralyzed from the neck down. Shaw proved them wrong again by slowly regaining the use of his upper torso through a series of operations. Now, he'd heard, the former pitcher would soon be facing yet another necessary surgery in an attempt to aid him in getting back the use of his legs.

Mike indicated the area beyond the batting cage, where parents were already congregating. "I'll just meander onto the field, mingle in with some of the dads." Talking to them would give him some background color for his story, he thought.

She nodded. She wanted to see if her father needed anything. This was the third time they were getting together—sessions were after school on Wednesdays and on Saturday mornings—and a routine was setting in. But since her father was doing this at her behest, she wanted to be available to him.

"Good luck," she told Mike, turning to go.

"Thanks. And Miranda—"

She stopped, peering at Mike over her shoulder. "Yes?"

He grinned and his eyes seemed to soften, pulling her in…and doing a number on her stomach. "Thanks for doing this."

She hardened herself against the effects of his handsome face. And pretty much failed, to her dismay. "Don't thank me yet," she warned. "I'm doing this because I believe in my father. You write one word that makes him unhappy, that puts him in an unflattering light and I'll—"

"Cut my heart out, right, I've got the picture." Rather than promise, he merely smiled again.

While she found him infinitely charming and definitely difficult to resist, it didn't abate her concerns. She wanted his word that he would give her father the respect he deserved.

"As long as you know," she said, walking off across the grass.

Mike smiled to himself as he watched her struggle not to sink into the softened earth. The woman needed a pair of sneakers, he thought as he went to join the other spectators.

But then, just before he reached his destination, Mike had a change of heart. He decided that since he was here, he might as well listen to what a once revered pitcher had to say to a bunch of nine- and ten-year-olds. Mike managed to position himself so that he was able to overhear a good deal.

It surprised Mike to discover that the once great pitcher did not treat the players as children or as disposable instruments, but as individuals. As people. Shaw referred to each of them, male and female alike, by the numbers that were stitched in below the team logo.

Voted most valuable player three years in a row, Shaw had never been any good at remembering names.

"Let me see that clipboard," Shaw said to Miranda, holding out his hand without looking in her direction. Eager for instruction, the team had all gathered around him.

Miranda carefully placed the clipboard into his hand. On the top sheet were all his dictated notes on which child was to play what position for the day.

While he believed in winning, Steven didn't believe children should be pushed to win at all costs, not at this stage. They still needed to have fun as they attempted to find their own personal place in the overall scheme of things.

Leaving the clipboard in his hand, Miranda stepped back. The space she'd vacated was immediately filled by two of the team members, both of whom squirmed to find their names on the sheet. They crowded the others who protested. Steven didn't have to say a word, he merely looked at the offending two and they instantly re-treated.

Miranda smiled to herself. God, did that bring back memories. It had been the same way with her and her sister whenever they squabbled or tried to best each other. Her father never had to verbally discipline them. All it took was that look and they were on their best behavior.

Lord but she missed Ariel. And the way things used to be.

"Here's the batting lineup for today," Steven announced in his soft, deep voice. "Number twelve is first," he said, glancing at a tall boy with a lopsided grin. "Then number eight, followed by number three…"

He continued down the line until everyone was accounted for. Next, he read off the positions they were to play.

Rather than announce it first, the way Mike would have thought he would, SOS kept the position of pitcher for last. Mike decided it was because to Shaw, the pitcher was—and probably always had been—the plum position.

"Okay." Steven held out the clipboard to his side for Miranda. She was quick to step up and take back the board. "Any questions?" Her father slowly scanned the sea of faces. No one raised their hand. He nodded his head, signaling an end to the huddle. "Then let's show them what we're made of."

The other team was batting first, so Steven's team took to the field, accompanied by several of the fathers, who were acting as umpires and secondary base coaches. Steven had already gone over which father went where before he addressed the players. Mike noted that the older men looked as eager as their kids to please Shaw.

Without any effort whatsoever, Steven Shaw seemed to cast an aura, leaving all who came in contact with the quiet-spoken man in complete awe.

Miranda moved away again, leaving her father to concentrate. She knew that look. He was weighing and measuring each of the players' strengths. She couldn't have been more thrilled. This was so much better for him than just sitting around in his yard, watching his life pass by with the wind.

"So, you think they're any good?"

Miranda's mouth dropped open as she realized too late that Mike had just walked up to her father. She'd thought the sportswriter would have observed longer than a few minutes before pouncing. Secretly, she'd been hoping that Mike's silent observation would last the entire session since it was his first time.

Her stomach tightened in anticipation. Miranda held her breath as her father glanced at the man who'd asked him the question, then looked back on the field, his attention focused on his team.

"I think there's potential here."

It was a guarded answer and so typical of her father, she thought. He'd never been the kind to lavish praise, but he also wasn't the type to heap criticism on a person, either, no matter what the age. And he never volunteered unless asked.

Mike decided to push the envelope a little, see what Shaw's response was. "You're not just saying that because you think it's something we want to hear?"

He was lumping himself in with the fathers, she realized, feeling somewhat relieved, even though her conscience pinched a bit. At least Marlowe was going along with the ruse for the time being.

Steven spared him a glance. "What would be the point?" he asked simply.

Mike grinned, nodding. "I guess you're right. What made you agree to do this?" Slipping his hands into his back pockets, he seemed without a care in the world, just a man shooting the breeze with a Little League coach. "I wouldn't know where to begin," he admitted, looking over toward the playing field.

"Not exactly rocket science," Steven told him. Just a hint of a smile curved his lips. The next moment, it was gone. "And my daughter thought I needed to get out more. She's the one with the clipboard hovering behind me," he added, nodding his head back in Miranda's general direction. "I think you've already met."

For form's sake, Mike glanced back at her. "Yes, in the parking lot," he acknowledged smoothly. He nodded at Miranda, as if to say hi. "Everyone needs a guardian angel."

Miranda was grateful to be standing behind her father so that he wouldn't see her cheeks go pink. Marlowe was right, she'd never pass for a spy.

Steven snorted. "The existence of those is highly debatable." And then he paused for a second, watching the other team's second batter swing at the pitch after the fact. It was his second miss, done in identical fashion. "Keep your eye on the pitcher's arm, not the ball," Steven told him. The boy looked at him with wide eyes. "You see it coming at you, it's already too late to swing. You start swinging a second before he releases."

The batter, gangly and nervous, nodded his head up and down like a bobble-head figurine.

"Isn't that seen as aiding and abetting the enemy?" Mike asked, amused and, at the same time, impressed that the man was willing to give advice to someone not on his team.

It was obvious that Steven didn't agree with his supposed take on the situation. "It's helping a kid not feel any worse about himself than he already does."

Mike laughed softly. "Wish you'd been around when I was trying out for the Little League team. I could have really used you."

Steven merely nodded, as if he was taking in just another stray piece of information. And then the man appraised him for a long moment. Mike had a feeling that he was being weighed and measured, just like the kids on the team.

"I've already assigned all the coaching positions," Steven told him matter-of-factly.

Mike looked out on the field. Every base had a father in close proximity and there were a couple more out in the field, as well.

"Yeah, I can see that. I'm not here for a position, I just thought I'd see how close I could get to a living legend." It was the truth in a manner of speaking. Mike was surprised to see a dark look descend over the former pitcher's face.

Scowling, Steven turned his attention back to the players. "You're in the wrong place for that. No living legends here, just a man trying to give a little something back."

At that moment, the boy he'd just coached finally made contact with the ball. The baseball flew in a high arc overhead, gaining more altitude than distance. Steven leaned forward, watching as two of his infielders ran in from separate points toward the ball. Both appeared to be watching the ball and were oblivious of each other.

They collided, falling to the ground amid groans. A fraction of a second before they did, the shortstop ran back, stretching his arm up overhead as far as it would go.

Miranda regretted not having a camera with her to capture the look of pure amazement, then joy when the boy saw that the ball was nestled in his glove. And that he had been the one to catch it.

"That one," Steven said, leaning back in his chair again, "has more than just potential." He nodded, as if conferring with himself. "That one has instincts and you can't teach that."

"Way to go, Robbie!" a father shouted from the side-lines.

"And he's also got a cheering section," Miranda commented with a smile.

"That's important, too," Mike heard himself adding. He remembered how Kate had demanded that his father take time out of his overwhelmingly busy schedule to watch his brothers and him play. He remembered, too, how angry she'd become with his father when, despite her urgings, he had failed to show up for one of the earlier games. His father had still been her employer at the time, but that hadn't stopped Kate from standing up to him for what she believed was right.

For them, he thought. He glanced at the man in the wheelchair, marveling at the twists and turns life took. Who would have ever thought that he'd actually meet the man he had once worshipped? Or that he'd find some common ground?

"You remind me a little of my stepmother," Mike confessed.

Steven glanced over at him. Mike couldn't begin to guess what the man was thinking. Was he insulted? Amused? Or just annoyed?

"She have a deep voice, too?" Steven finally asked him.

"No, just a deep-seated sense of integrity," Mike replied honestly. He hesitated for a moment, then he asked, "Do you mind if I just hover around for a bit, watching you?"

"I'd rather you didn't hover—" And then he shrugged, as if rethinking the dismissal. "But you can take a seat on the bench when our team bats if you want. I don't have a batboy," Steven remarked, not that he had planned on filling that position. It was more for show in professional games than an actual necessity. "You can hand out bats to the players before they get up to take their turn in the cage."

Mike didn't bother hiding the grin that came to his lips. He had to admit, part of him felt like a kid again. "Yes, sir."

Steven waved his hand dismissively at the term he'd just used. "Coach'll do."

Truer words had never been spoken. Mike went to drag over the canvas duffel bag filled with baseball bats.

"Do you realize that you've been grinning for two hours now?" Miranda noted when Mike worked his way over to her.

The game was over and they were packing up. Their team had won by two runs, thanks more to errors on the part of the other team. Mike was gathering up the equipment that Steven had brought with him in the van.

His grin only widened at her comment. "I think being here like this tapped into the inner kid in me," Mike confessed. He stopped and looked around. In the distance, parents gathered up their kids and cars pulled out of the lot. It was dark and the artificial lights were on, but no one seemed to notice. There seemed to be an electrical charge in the air. "This wasn't what I expected," he admitted.

Miranda had volunteered to bring the after-game snacks and was collecting the drinks and granola bars that hadn't been eaten. She stopped packing them away and looked at him, curious for more than one reason. "What did you expect?"

"I'm not sure. A little of the killer instinct on display, I guess. A former player I knew, Jim Bishop—he played in the minors for a few years—never seemed to have what it took to reach the majors. But he trained the kids on his team as if they were getting ready for the pros. He barked orders and threw around insults whenever his team didn't play up to his expectations. And I won't even go into what he said about the players on the other team. They didn't let him coach the following year. There were too many complaints from the parents."

And he thought that her father was going to be like that? Her protectiveness flared up and she banked it down as best she could.

"Little men with something to prove do that," Miranda told him coolly. She narrowed her eyes. "My father doesn't feel he has anything to prove—or apologize for," she emphasized, throwing the last in for good measure.

That brought them back full circle to the subject of Steven's permanent ban from baseball. But Mike didn't want to think about that right now—or delve into the principles he'd quoted so religiously in the initial article that had brought Miranda into his life. He wanted to savor what he'd just experienced.

Mike'd found himself really liking the man. He wanted to enjoy having spent part of an afternoon with the man who had once been his hero.

"No, he certainly doesn't have anything to prove," Mike agreed.

She was a scientist and it was in her nature to examine things, including words. She heard what Mike was saying, as well as what he wasn't saying, thereby delivering his message loud and clear.

After bundling up the leftover snacks, she tossed them into a double-lined garbage bag and yanked hard on the red tie.

Maybe this wasn't such a great idea after all. When was she going to learn that she just couldn't trust everyone without limits? Just because Mike Marlowe sounded sincere and professed having been a dedicated fan didn't mean he would give her father a fair shake in his article.

Mike reached over to help her with the bag and she pulled it out of his reach. She didn't need his damn help.

Miranda squared her shoulders. "He doesn't have

anything to apologize for, either," she informed him in a low, firm voice before she turned on her heel and quickly walked away from him.

Chapter Seven

Miranda held her breath the next morning as she opened the newspaper to the sports section…and then released it after she'd read Mike's column. There was no mention of her father.

No news was good news, right? And, after all, what had transpired yesterday on the field hadn't exactly been an interview. It was more like a semiconversation between the two men.

She'd been close enough to hear what was said. There hadn't been anything in the discussion that Mike could report as offensive. She knew that didn't stop some journalists, but she was holding Mike to his word.

When she found nothing in his column about her father on the second day, or the third, she began to wonder if Marlowe had decided to give up the idea of writing about Steven Shaw, good or bad. That wasn't what she'd wanted, either, although "nothing" was preferable to a bad "something."

By lunchtime on the fifth day, she couldn't contain her curiosity. Promise Pharmaceuticals not only had a cafeteria for their employees, but also provided shaded tables on a wide terrace facing the back of the building. She took her lunch there and removed Mike's folded napkin from her wallet. Time to get in touch.

It took two tries to reach him. The first went to voice mail. Though impatient, she forced herself to wait until she was finished eating before trying the cell-phone number again. This time, she would leave a message.

She didn't have to. Mike picked up just before the recorded message kicked in.

"This is Mike." His baritone voice rumbled against her ear. His declaration was punctuated by the sound of a female voice laughing in the background.

Well, that certainly explained why she hadn't been able to get him before, Miranda thought.

"Am I interrupting something?" she asked him, struggling to keep the coolness out of her voice.

"Miranda?"

"Yes." She should have just hung up instead of saying anything. For reasons she couldn't pin down, she felt like an idiot now.

"Hi." He sounded happy to hear from her. Obviously the man had hidden acting talent. "Wait just a second. Hey, guys," she heard him say to someone in the background, "keep it down, will you? This is business."

"Business." Now there was a female voice echoing his word back at him coyly. "Is that what you call it now, Mikey?"

Miranda had no idea why that comment annoyed her. Both the coy tone the woman used and the fact that she, Miranda, was "business."

Well, what else would she be? she silently demanded, irritated. *You know you wouldn't be comfortable if it was anything else. You wouldn't have called him if this wasn't about "business."*

At least with Mike it was more clear-cut. For most of her life, people had tried to garner her friendship in order to get autographs or tickets to a sold-out ball game. She found out who her true friends were after the gambling scandal. The ones who no longer called her had been there under false pretenses. Tilda was among the very small number who remained loyal and trustworthy no matter what. As for Mike, could she trust him even if it was just business?

"Sorry," Mike apologized. By the sudden stillness in the background, she guessed that he had to have gone to another room to talk to her. "My sister's at that weird age where she thinks everything out of her mouth is witty."

"Your sister?" Miranda realized she was smiling. Why should it matter to her whether or not he was with another woman?

"Yes, my sister. Kelsey. You've reached me at my parents' house. I've got the day off and—" He stopped himself midexplanation. "Well, you didn't call to hear a bunch of personal stuff. What can I do for you?"

She cleared her throat, focusing. "I was just wondering why you didn't write anything in your column about my father. It's been five days. Did you change your mind?"

"Hell, no," he said with feeling. "I didn't write anything because I didn't interview him yet. I want to talk to him at least a few more times before I put an article together."

Then he *did* want to do an interview. That was both good and bad, she thought, feeling ambivalent again. "So are you going to tell him that you're interviewing him?" she asked.

"It's only ethical. But I think I'd be better off doing it after I get him to like me a little," he added. She could almost see the way his grin spread out over his face. "Don't worry, I won't implicate you."

"But he saw us talking," she reminded him.

"Dozens of reasons for that," Mike told her. "Not the least of which is my trying to get your number to ask you out." He paused for a moment, as if waiting for her to say something. When she didn't, he forged on. "Speaking of which, what are you doing next Sunday afternoon?"

She thought for a second, her mind suddenly a blank. "Um, having brunch with a friend." Barring something unforeseeable, she and Tilda had a standing date at 10:00 a.m.

"Oh."

Was that a tinge of disappointment in his voice? Or just fanciful thinking on her part? In either case, she heard herself clarifying, "A girlfriend," for absolutely no good reason.

"Oh." This time the word sounded a great deal brighter. It *wasn't* her imagination. "Would your girl-friend mind if you postponed it?"

Air stopped in her lungs. "Why would I do that?"

"My parents are having an anniversary party on Sunday—their anniversary's really the following Tuesday, but we can't all make it at that time so they're having the party on Sunday. Anyway, I thought that maybe, if you weren't doing anything... Look, if this is the slightest bit awkward for you, then never mind. I understand."

She took a breath. "And if it's not awkward for me...?" she hypothesized.

"Then I'd like you to come."

"To your parents' house?" she asked in disbelief.

"Yes. It's a barbecue. You do eat meat?" he asked suddenly.

"I eat meat," she assured him.

Well, this was certainly different than being lured to a man's apartment for an evening of covert seduction. She had to admit that she was attracted to Mike. What safer place to see him than in his home setting? Besides, she could learn a few things, watching him interact with his family.

"And your parents won't mind my crashing their an-niversary party?"

"You won't be crashing, you'll be coming with me," he pointed out.

That meant he didn't have a girlfriend, she realized. Her pulse accelerated just a tad. "Do you mind if I think about it?"

Everything inside her shouted "yes" but she had to be cautious. Impulse had gotten her into a couple of relationships that had soured without warning, hurting her after she'd invested a large chunk of herself. For all she knew, this could have just been Mike's way of thanking her for putting him in touch with her father.

"Sure," he said, "but it's all aboveboard. And if you find that you're not having a good time, just tell me and I promise I'll take you home. What could be more fair than that?" he coaxed.

"Nothing," she admitted, and then she laughed softly to herself. "I'll say this for you, you know how to mount a good argument."

"My father's a lawycr, and so is one of my brothers. Maybe it's in the blood, like a latent gene," he speculated.

Or maybe it was just pure charm, she thought. The man certainly had it to spare. She could all but envision the expression on his face right at this moment.

"That would explain it," she allowed. Oh, what the hell? "Okay, I'll come."

"Great."

He sounded genuinely happy to hear her decision. She tried not to let her mind get carried away. This was just going to be a sociable afternoon, nothing more.

No matter how appealing his mouth seemed.

"I need to know what to wear," she began. Did that sound as mindlessly lame as she thought? She didn't want him to think she was a fashion diva. "I mean, is it casual, or—"

"I'll give you all the details Wednesday," he promised.

"Wednesday?" she echoed.

"Yes, on the field," he reminded her. "Your father's going to be coaching his team tomorrow, right?"

"Right."

Was that his angle? she suddenly wondered. To make her father think that he was interested in her so that his constant questions would seem normal? Was he using her after all?

"Okay, then I'll see you there," he said, winding down the conversation. "'Bye," he said, before hanging up.

Miranda sat for a moment, looking at the cell phone in her hand. What had just happened? Had she just agreed to a date—or a setup?

"You look as if you don't know if you should laugh or cry."

Miranda glanced up and saw that Tilda was crossing over to her table. Their usual lunch routine was broken today because Tilda had to make a quick run to the bank.

Miranda rose to her feet, falling into step beside her friend as Tilda continued on to the back entrance of the building.

"Funny, that's just exactly how I feel." And confused as hell, she added silently.

Tilda smiled with not-so-hidden amusement. "Does this have anything to do with that cute sportswriter?"

The question took her by surprise. "How do you know he's cute? You've never met him."

"Not in person, no," Tilda agreed. "Okay, the guy

who writes the sports column and takes good pictures—that accurate enough for you? And by your evasive answer," she continued with her deduction, "I take that as a yes. So, are you going out with him?"

"In a manner of speaking," Miranda answered. And then she smiled as she shook her head. "Maybe you should take up mind reading."

"Maybe I should." Walking in front of her, Tilda pushed one of the heavy glass doors open and walked into the cool building. The temperature was never very high inside, even in the dead of one of their colder winters. Warm temperatures affected the outcome of experiments. "It would certainly give me a lot more answers than you are these days."

Miranda followed. The glass door swung shut behind her. She felt bad about being evasive with her best friend, but then, she was being evasive with herself, as well. "He invited me to a family party."

Tilda stopped in midstep and turned around. "When did it get serious?"

Okay, so now she was going to pay for being too honest and open. "It didn't."

"Yes, it did," Tilda insisted, lowering her voice. "There's family involved."

Miranda shrugged. "Maybe he believes in the philosophy of 'I'll show you mine and then you show me yours.'"

Tilda bit back a laugh as she resumed walking again. They turned down a long corridor. "We are still talking about family, aren't we?"

Miranda took a breath, opening the door to the lab

where they spent a large portion of their days. Apparently they were the first ones back from lunch.

"Yes, we are," she told Tilda firmly. "I don't know, maybe Marlowe thinks that I'll be less protective of my father if he shows me how he interacts with his own family."

Tilda seemed far from convinced. Her scientific mind had its limits. "Miranda, sometimes there's such a thing as overthinking."

Miranda slipped on the white lab coat she'd left draped over the back of her chair. "Meaning?"

"Maybe the guy just wants to get lucky and since you're obviously such a daddy's girl—you are, you know, whether you admit it or not—he thinks that the way to get to you is to show you how close he is to his."

Wow, talk about convoluted, Miranda thought. "Now who's overthinking things? And for your information," she added, "Marlowe's not going to 'get lucky.'"

Tilda took her seat at her desk. Genuine regret came over her features. "Now that's a shame."

"Why?" Miranda demanded.

"Because, dear friend, that means that neither are you."

Miranda opened her mouth to deny there was anything going on between her and Marlowe, then closed it again. There were times when retreating was the only way to handle things. She just wasn't going to convince Tilda of her platonic relationship with the good-looking sportswriter so there was no point in fighting a losing battle.

"Guess not," she murmured in agreement as she turned her attention to her latest experiment.

"Like I said, a real shame."
Miranda pretended not to hear.

Miranda had absolutely no intentions of "getting lucky." Tilda's words still echoed in her head Wednesday afternoon as she pulled her car into the school parking lot. Much to her disappointment, she'd discovered a few years ago that like most mythical creatures, sex had been assigned a whole litany of attributes it just didn't possess.

Granted she hadn't had that many partners, only three actually, but she'd never once heard bells ringing, or music playing, and never seen fireworks go off before or during sex. The so-called out-of-body experience never happened for her—and she'd been in love with each of her partners. She did know that the anticipation of lovemaking for the first time with each was always far more exciting than the actual consummation.

If—and it was a huge "if"—it ever got to that point with Marlowe, she knew that history would just repeat itself.

But even as she reasoned with herself, a warmth slipped over her the moment she spotted Mike. He'd obviously arrived early and was already on the field. She saw him carefully lining up the bats by the bench behind the batting cage.

He was talking to her father.

Watching them, she felt torn and more than a little conflicted. Part of her wanted to tell her father who Mike really was, while the other part of her thought that this interaction with another man was good for him.

Even from this distance, her father finally seemed to

be opening up. Oh, not like the average man who might just go on and on about something once the right buttons were pressed. In her father's case, saying more than two or three words was a huge accomplishment.

Obviously Marlowe was good at what he did, she thought, closing up her car. She still watched the two of them as she crossed the field. Maybe it was a good thing she was going to this family celebration with him on Sunday. Who knew? Watching the way a person interacted with his own family would give her valuable insight into the man she had inadvertently allowed into her father's life.

More than that, it would indicate if she was making a mistake by trusting him.

"Hi, Dad," she called out the moment she was within earshot. Because she'd made it a point to leave work early today, she had the time to actually dress more appropriately for a game. Instead of high heels and a skirt and blouse, she wore sneakers and jeans along with a royal blue hoodie she left unzipped. The light blue T-shirt she had on beneath had seen more than its share of spin cycles.

She saw Mike turn toward her and felt his eyes pass over her, taking inventory. An appreciative look came into them. The heat rose to her cheeks. She silently cursed the fact that she was so light-skinned. Her father's complexion was almost bronzed from all the time he'd always spent out in the sun. She took after her mother and right now really wished she didn't.

Mike waved at her. "Hi."

"Hi," she murmured back, nodding her head. Feeling

a bit self-conscious, she focused her attention on her father, deliberately turning her head away from Mike. "It's kind of chilly, Dad. Shouldn't you be wearing a warmer jacket?"

"Only if I wanted to," he replied. He was busy looking over a list of notes on his clipboard. In the distance, cars had begun arriving, depositing children in uniforms.

Putting down the last bat, Mike looked over in her direction. "I think your dad's old enough to make decisions for himself."

When did this happen? When had Mike joined Team Shaw and when did she get kicked off?

"I'm not implying he can't make his own decisions—I'm not, Dad," she said with feeling, glancing at him. "I just worry about you."

She saw the faintest of smiles on her father's lips. "Doesn't do any good, does it?" he asked simply.

"No." She sighed, giving in. Nobody could ever get her father to do anything he didn't want to do. That had always been a given. "It doesn't."

"Then why do it?" Steven asked.

Miranda shrugged. "I guess that I'm just made that way."

"It's kind of nice," Mike interjected, this time addressing his words to her father, "having someone care enough to worry about you."

Out of the corner of her eye, she saw her father nodding in agreement. Marlowe was incredible, she thought. Without any effort at all, he was playing both sides of the field. And managing to score points for each team.

Chapter Eight

"I think you're getting your wish," she said to Mike when he picked her up the following Sunday afternoon at her apartment.

He smiled at her seductively. "Which wish would that be?"

Miranda suddenly had trouble swallowing. Her hands tightened around the bouquet of flowers she held. What would it be like to feel those lips against hers?

It wasn't easy, talking with her breath backing up in her lungs, but she managed. "About getting my father to like you."

Mike opened the passenger-side door for her and waited until she got in. After he closed the door, he went around the rear of his vehicle. Sitting down behind the steering wheel, he pulled the seat belt around him.

"You've got my undivided attention," he told her. "But then—" he smiled at her again "—you already had that."

They were just lines, she told herself. Lines a man used to get a woman to lower her defenses.

And were they ever working.

"I talked to him last night, just to make sure he was okay, and he mentioned you."

Mike pulled out of the parking space and made his way out of the apartment complex. "Do you do that often?" he asked.

"Do what?" she asked, confused.

A blue SUV tore past him, narrowly avoiding clipping the nose of his car. Mike swore silently in his head, then composed himself.

"Call to check on him," he answered. "Your father doesn't strike me as being in particularly bad condition. I mean, other than the fact that he's in a wheelchair and can't walk."

Without thinking, she held the bouquet closer to her, as if that could somehow contain the emotions churning inside her. "I almost lost him during the last operation—he's had several so far. His heart stopped beating," she continued. "The doctor said it took two attempts to get it going again." She blew out a breath. Even talking about it made her throat tighten up. "I don't take a single thing for granted when it comes to my father. He's all the family I have."

They stopped at a light and Miranda caught herself

studying his profile. Marlowe was more complicated than she'd thought.

"Why aren't you asking what he said about you?" she finally asked. "Aren't you curious?"

The light changed and Mike took his foot off the brake, but not before he glanced at her. "Yes," he freely admitted, "but when it comes to your father, I'm curious about everything, including his relationship with you."

A small laugh escaped her lips. Nobody was interested in a woman who spent her days trying to break down proteins and synthesize cures for illusive diseases. "*That* would make for very boring reading," she assured him.

There it was again, that smile that curled straight into her stomach. She felt poised at the top of a thirty-foot roller-coaster drop, one second before descent.

"Why don't you let me be the judge of that?" he suggested smoothly.

"Besides," she insisted, deliberately looking at the bouquet rather than his face, "it doesn't have anything to do with the price of tomatoes." Glancing up, she saw a slight frown slip over his mouth. "My life has nothing to do with getting the ban against my father rescinded."

Mike shook his head. "We have a difference of opinion there. I'm trying to deal with the whole man, not just the icon, and you're very much a part of that." Getting comfortable, he shared his approach with her. "If I get the feel for the whole person, I can pass that onto my readers. It'll make them feel as if they're really getting to know him." He made a sharp right turn, narrowly avoiding missing it. "Are you and your father close?"

"Not exactly. We've slowly become closer since

the accident, but I don't think that my father can actually *be* close to anyone," she admitted with regret. "He had a very hard upbringing. From what I gathered, his parents believed that displays of emotion were equivalent to being weak. In order to please them, he was stoic. It became a habit he couldn't break." And she hated that invisible barrier that always seemed to separate them. "He kept everything inside—except that one time when my sister died." She realized she was repeating herself. "But I already told you about that."

"I don't mind hearing it again." He sounded so sincere, she almost believed him. "I was the type of kid who liked to hear the same story night after night—gave me a sense of stability and continuity, I guess." He saw the amused expression on her face. "What?"

"Me, too," she admitted, surprised that they had that in common. "There were three stories I had my mother read to me every single night before she went on to anything new. Drove her and my sister crazy," she recalled.

Miranda enjoyed dipping into the past for a minute. Remembering the good times. Because the bad times cast such a large, dark shadow she tended to forget about the happier moments.

"My sister was the daredevil in the family. For her, everything had to be new, exciting. In their own way, both my parents got a real kick out of her. I think Dad saw a lot of himself in her—and so did my mother." She paused for a second, trying to come to terms with the pain. "After Ariel died, everything changed. Everything in the house was so quiet, like a church where everyone's lost in prayer."

Her words replayed themselves in her head. She blinked, eyeing him in wonder. "How did I wind up talking about this? Tell me about your family," she coaxed, settling back.

"You planning on writing an article about them?" he deadpanned.

"I'm just looking for a fair exchange of information." She glanced down at the flowers and realized her error. "Like I hope your stepmother's not allergic to roses."

He thought of Kate. "Even if she were, she wouldn't let on. She's that kind of a person. Doesn't ever want to hurt anyone's feelings for any reason. I can't think of a single person who doesn't like her." He smiled, remembering the first time he'd ever seen her, at one of his friends' birthday parties. Kate had been hired to entertain them and she was conducting a puppet show. "She certainly fixed our world."

Miranda waited, but he didn't follow up and explain. "You're going to have to give me more than that, Marlowe."

"Okay." He slanted a glance at her and nodded. But just as he was about to continue, he stopped. "I will if you will."

"Not much more to tell you than I already have," she said, sounding as innocent as she could. She wouldn't relay her father's one low point shortly after he'd come home from the hospital, when he'd tried to end it all himself. And he would have, if she hadn't come in when she had. She'd called a trusted family doctor and persuaded him to make a house call—and then begged him not to tell the police. Her father's eyes were devoid of emotion when they opened the next day. But in time, though he never said it in so many words, he was thankful that she'd kept him from killing himself.

"Now, just how did your stepmother manage to fix your world?" she prodded.

"My mother died in a plane crash. My father couldn't really cope with coming home and not seeing her there so he threw himself into his work—even more than he already had. That's what they used to argue about, that he was spending too much time at work. He always told her it was because she spent money faster than he could earn it. The nannies he hired just weren't up to a set of triplets and a cocky six-year-old."

"I take it that the cocky six-year-old was you."

He laughed, taking another sharp right. "Guilty as charged. We went through three nannies in short order—maybe four. And then my dad found Kate. She wasn't really a nanny, but a student trying to earn extra money on the side by doing kids' parties. She was— is—a ventriloquist. Impressed with the way she handled a bunch of six-year-olds, my father cornered her before she could leave and offered her a job."

Miranda smiled. "And the rest is history?"

"No," he countered, "Kate turned him down at first. But then her tuition and her rent went up and she was really strapped for money. Being our nanny meant she could have free room and board, as well as a salary— my father was *really* desperate—so she said yes."

Mike drove by a mall that hadn't been there when

he and his brothers were growing up in the neighborhood. Things had really changed, he thought. "We weren't easy on her. God knew we came with our own special baggage even at that age, but she stuck it out, found a way to bring out the best in us, and along the way, she made us whole again. Made us a family again. Especially after Dad proposed to her." His smile widened. "They've been together for twenty years now and Dad still worships the ground she walks on."

Miranda tried to imagine what that was like, having parents who openly cared about one another. All she remembered was the silence, the lack of communication. "Must be nice having parents who love each other that much."

"Your parents didn't?"

Miranda shrugged, helpless to change a past that had left its mark her. "Like I said, my father wasn't the kind who opened up. Oh, he did what he could, brought presents and took us places when he was home, but he was gone a good six to eight months out of the year. I guess in retrospect he was more of a lover than a husband to my mother. I don't doubt they loved each other once, but the lasting, familiar, comfortable kind of love, that they didn't have," she lamented.

"When he was home, he didn't know where anything went, how things were done from day to day, things like that. He was a stranger in his own home and he resented it. Meanwhile, my mother resented him trying to take over after not being around. After a while, my parents realized they were just two strangers living under the same roof for a few months out of the year."

She took a deep breath, steeling herself. "And then Ariel died and things just fell apart. They both went to their separate corners to grieve." She remembered how cold it seemed then. How there was no one to turn to because they had both withdrawn into themselves. "Mom divorced Dad and just kept slipping into this netherworld where nothing and no one could get through to her. She died a little more than eighteen months after Ariel did."

She could remember having to tell her father the news. It was one of the most awful moments of her life. He didn't say anything for a long time, so long that she'd thought he'd just hung up. He came the next day to take her home with him and make the funeral arrangements.

"Dad kept pushing on, doing the only thing he knew how, play baseball. And then that scandal erupted." Around this time she began to think her family was cursed.

"Does it make any sense for your father to jeopardize everything by getting involved with a known gambling ring?" Mike asked her suddenly.

She wondered this herself, going over it in the dead of night when all things were at their bleakest.

"Completely out of character," she said. "But then, grief can make a person do strange things, I guess." It was the only explanation she had. After all, her father never contested the charges. "And then the accident happened. A drunk driver crashed into him one night a few months after he was banned from baseball. I didn't think things could get any worse." Although they had, she added silently.

He wondered if she was privy to the rumors, or if

she'd heard and just chose to shut them out. "A lot of people thought SOS was trying to commit suicide that night."

"He wasn't," she retorted fiercely. "He wouldn't have done that to Ariel's memory—or to me."

At least, she added silently, not then.

As a writer, he was acutely aware of the way words were used. "Shouldn't that be worded the other way around?"

"No." She wished it could, but that would only be lying to herself. She had made peace with the truth. "I knew he liked Ariel better. Both my parents liked Ariel better," she said simply. "So did I, really," she admitted with a rueful smile. "Ariel was fun, and cool and just so full of life. Everyone loved being around her."

Miranda paused for a moment, staring out through the windshield at the neatly manicured trees passing by. Wishing things had turned out differently. But they hadn't.

She was acutely aware of Mike watching her.

"My mother got annoyed over something I did not long after Ariel's funeral—I can't remember what it was, something dumb probably…" She waved her hand, dismissing whatever it had been. "And I heard her say under her breath, 'You should have been the one who died, not my Ariel.'"

Mike saw her bite her lower lip, as if trying to contain the sadness the memory had raised.

Miranda felt self-conscious. If they weren't in a moving vehicle, she would have probably turned on her heel and walked away.

"I've never told anyone that before." She let out a long, shaky breath fraught with tears she refused to *ever* shed and looked over at him. "You really are good at drawing things out of people."

Mike tried to put himself in her place, tried to imagine how it felt to know that someone she loved wished she had died in her sister's place. He couldn't even begin to fathom it. He'd felt alone when his mother died, but he'd always shared his grief with his brothers. His father had distanced himself from them. And the four of them, despite the fact that they were all very young, had taken solace in one another. He'd never truly been alone, the way Miranda must have felt.

For the first time, he saw her as a whole person. Not just the extremely attractive daughter of a one-time major league icon. She was a woman whose life was layered.

He felt himself reacting to what she'd said. Reacting to her.

Taking a final right turn, he pulled up into a spot fortuitously located right next to his parents' driveway. "I'm sorry, Miranda."

"For making me talk?" she guessed, a whimsical smile playing along her lips. Her eyes stung and she tried fervently to combat the emotions by grinning broadly.

He glanced at her again and found himself struggling with the desire to take her in his arms and hold her. To comfort her even though he knew it was beyond his actual ability to do so.

"No, for causing you to dig up memories that are obviously very painful."

She laughed shortly. "Just doing your job, right?" Before he could make any comment on her assessment, Miranda nodded toward an inviting blue-and-gray house. "Shouldn't we be getting out of the car?" she asked. "Or does your family have curbside service?"

Mike let the subject go for now. At the same time, he filed away the look he had seen on Miranda's face. For a moment, Miranda's vulnerability had been exposed and he'd felt both guilty for having brought it about and protective of her.

Not that she would welcome the latter, he mused. From what he'd witnessed so far, Steven Orin Shaw's daughter was a very independent, self-possessed young woman. Exposing her vulnerable side probably caused her no small amount of embarrassment.

It wasn't something he wanted to capitalize on, just soothe. Maybe it was his knight-in-shining-armor side rising to the surface.

Getting out of the vehicle, Mike rounded the hood and came up to the passenger door. But Miranda had already opened her side and she was in the process of swinging out her legs. The black-and-white checkered skirt she wore climbed high on her thighs. A wave of warmth swept over him as he took in the sight. Damn, but she had one hell of a set of legs. They alone could bring a man to his knees.

Mike offered her his hand and she politely ignored it. Standing up and clearing the vehicle, she clutched her bouquet, holding it in front of her like a good-luck talisman.

The front door swung open as they made their way

up the walk. Their path was buffered on both sides by fragrant rosebushes sporting yellow buds that had obviously gotten their seasons confused, a common malady for flowers in Southern California.

A petite woman, her bouncy blond hair cut short, held the door wide-open. The smile on her flawless face was wide and welcoming.

"Last one here, as always," Kate informed her oldest son—she'd always hated the term *stepson,* maintaining that it made the boys seem like a step below the real thing. "But you brought company with you, so you're forgiven." Rising up on her toes, she brushed her lips against his cheek, then turned toward Miranda. If possible, her smile widened even more as she extended her hand to her unknown guest. "Hello, I'm Kate Marlowe."

"Miranda Shaw," Miranda responded, enveloping the offered hand.

The young woman's handshake was firm, Kate noted. She liked that. Her eyes shifted toward the bouquet Miranda held in her other hand.

"Those are lovely roses."

Miranda had almost forgotten she was holding them. Coming to, she thrust them at Kate. "They're for you," she said belatedly. "I didn't know what to bring," she confessed.

There was an endless fount of kindness in Kate's eyes. Miranda caught herself thinking that rarely had she ever seen a more sympathetic-looking woman. She liked her instantly.

Kate accepted the flowers with great pleasure. "Thank you very much, but you really didn't need to bring anything but yourself." She looked at Mike. "You didn't tell her it was our anniversary, did you?"

Mike gave her a quick, one-armed hug and kissed the top of her head. The affection between the two was obvious. "I didn't know it was a secret."

"Women feel obligated to bring something if they think it's an occasion," Kate informed him. Her tone indicated that she knew it was hopeless to think he might remember that the next time around. Kate looked back to Miranda. "You'll have to excuse Mike, he hasn't had all that much experience with women."

Mike feigned annoyance, as if his biggest secret had just been exposed. "Why don't you just post that on the Internet?"

"She might not, but I can," Trent volunteered, coming forward. His broad smile was for his brother's guest's benefit. "Hi, I'm—"

"One third of an annoying trio," Mike interrupted, taking her arm. "Why don't I take you to meet my father?" he suggested.

"—Trent," Trent called after her.

She laughed and waved at him as Mike ushered her through the sliding-glass door in the family room. "Hi, I'm Miranda."

Guiding her around several guests, Mike directed her toward the large silver barbecue grill. Clustered around it she saw two more people who looked exactly like the man who'd introduced himself as Trent.

Miranda's mouth dropped open. She'd seen the family photograph in Mike's wallet, but looking at his brothers in person had that much more of an impact on her. She would have never been able to tell them apart. And even Mike resembled them enough to be mistaken as a fraternal twin.

"They really are triplets," she murmured. She didn't realize Kate was directly behind her until she heard the woman laugh.

"The first time I met them, I asked their father if he worked for Xerox," Kate confessed. With the ease of an old friend, Kate slipped her arm through Miranda's.

The moment she did that, Miranda felt instantly at ease. And at home.

Chapter Nine

Miranda wasn't accustomed to fitting in easily anymore, certainly not without any effort on her part. Having learned early to treat overtures of friendship with caution, she was used to being on the outside looking in. And when people were *overly* friendly toward her, she had the uncomfortable feeling that they weren't interested in friendship, but in getting an inside track to her father.

To his credit, when she was young and asked her father for the autographs, photos or tickets, he would always come through. But even then, there'd be this enigmatic expression on his face. She realized later that it masked pity, for her having to trade on his name to get friends. Until she grew older she was in the dark about the way people operated. Oh, she had her suspicions, but she never actually acted on them. And so things continued the way they were. Even Ariel's death didn't really change things that much.

But then the scandal happened.

From then on, she became highly suspicious of anyone who even asked her about her family. It became ingrained in her. So ingrained she couldn't change her ways, couldn't just shed her wariness like some burdensome cocoon. After the scandal, instead of fans, she was periodically beset by reporters and by writers who wanted to do a biography on her father, or, occasionally, by baseball historians who wanted to ask SOS face-to-face, "What were you thinking?"

So, in a nutshell, Miranda was forever on her guard against exactly what Mike Marlowe represented—the prying media.

However, the Marlowes and their handful of friends didn't seem to care that much about baseball or her father's place in its history. After a while, she began to think that perhaps no one knew who her father was. They were being friendly to her because she was with Mike.

With Mike.

Miranda slanted a covert glance in his direction. He stood by the barbecue grill, talking rather animatedly to his father. He caught her looking and grinned before continuing his conversation.

With Mike.

God, that almost sounded as if they were a couple, and they weren't. Not even dating, she thought, ignoring the tinge of regret that accompanied that acknowledgment.

She'd come to the party to see him interact with his family and he'd brought her here to what…? Get her to let down her guard and trust him? She already did on some level because, if she didn't, no way would she have allowed him to meet her father.

Maybe Mike had seen the uneasiness reflected in her eyes, the uneasiness she felt because she thought maybe she'd made a mistake after all and *that* was why he'd decided to ask her to come with him to this family gathering. It didn't take an Einstein to see that she was very big on families.

But, whatever his reason for bringing her—and hers for coming—she couldn't deny one thing. His family made her feel as if she'd always been coming here. They'd absorbed her as if she was a part of them. No one regarded her as the "new kid on the block" or "odd woman out." They pulled her into conversations and sprinkled in just enough questions to get her to talk about herself. She became entrenched within their gathering—and loved it.

There was an easy camaraderie among them, Miranda quickly noted. At the center of it all was Kate. Maybe if Kate had been her mother, her father wouldn't have remained an island unto himself when Ariel died. If Kate had been her mother, her parents wouldn't have turned from each other and withdrawn into themselves, leaving her emotionally stranded.

But life was what it was. There was no point in wishing that things had been otherwise. For now she was just going to enjoy this family. Enjoy the fact that people like this actually existed. She'd begun to think that they didn't, that nothing but sadness littered the world.

She did a lot of laughing during the course of the afternoon and evening. The Marlowes were an entertaining lot and she quickly forgot to be on her guard.

It felt wonderful.

Time went by all too quickly. Soon it was dark and the people attending the barbecue adjourned to the family room, driven in by the cool evening air.

Conversations continued, overlapping one another, weaving themselves into a greater whole. Her opinion was asked on a dozen different matters, compared and contrasted, evaluated and approved.

Several times her head felt as if it was spinning as she tried to listen to several conversations at once, take in everything and add her two cents, as well.

"Had enough yet?" Mike asked, whispering the question close to her ear as he presented her with the piña colada his father had made just for her.

Miranda was perched on the arm of a cream-colored suede sofa. Taking the drink, she tried not to react, but the feel of Mike's warm breath along her neck evoked a deep-seated shiver down her spine. It raised her heart rate by a good twenty points.

She pretended to be focused on the drink, wrapping her fingers around the stem of the glass slowly. She wished with all her heart that she was more like her father. Emotion rarely registered on his face.

"I'm stuffed," she answered in reply.

"No, I meant have you had enough of them?" He nodded about the room, taking in the scattered members of his family. He noted that Miranda had eased herself out of the circles of conversation for a moment and he thought she wanted to leave.

She smiled and shook her head. She doubted if she could ever have enough of people like the Marlowes. She was content just to sit and listen.

"No, I haven't," she told him honestly. "I like them."

That, to him, was a given. Everyone liked his family.

"Thought you might," he responded. Taking a seat on the sofa, he tugged on her skirt, indicating that she join him.

She slid off the arm of the couch and found herself nestled in between the thick upholstered arm…and Mike's hard body. Something crackled through her like closely packed firecrackers. From experience she knew only disappointment lay ahead of her, but that didn't dampen the electrical charge racing through her veins.

Mike was acutely aware of the presence of his family. As much as he loved them, he wished they weren't here right now. Or, at the very least, that they were back out on the patio, or in the yard or even in the garage.

Anywhere but in this room.

Because he sensed that if he acted on his impulses, he'd never hear the end of it from his sister, Kelsey— and probably his brothers, as well. Not to mention Miranda was definitely not the type to kiss someone with an audience looking on.

Mike smiled. "They have a habit of growing on you,"

he said in response. He glanced at his watch. It was almost eleven. "But it is getting late and you've got work tomorrow."

If she didn't know any better, she would have said he sounded almost parental. A father shooing his daughter off to bed because "tomorrow was a school day." She looked at him, amused. "Don't you also have work?"

"My profession's a little more lax than yours," he told her. "I don't have to turn up at a specific time. As long as I e-mail my column to the sports editor before the day's deadline, I'm all right."

She scanned the room. Everyone was still here. "We'll be the first to leave," she pointed out.

"Someone has to be or this'll go on forever." With that, he stood up and took her hand. "C'mon," he coaxed, "just follow my lead."

She'd stayed a great deal longer than she'd originally intended—and wanted to stay even longer, but Mike was right. It was getting late and although she felt even more wide-awake now than she had when she'd first arrived, she'd regret it tomorrow. She wasn't a morning person. Not getting enough sleep would automatically turn her into a semifunctioning zombie on Monday morning.

"I had a wonderful time," she told Kate and Bryan as she and Mike said their goodbyes. "Thank you for having me."

"Anyone who can put up with Mike is more than welcome here," Bryan assured her, taking her hand between both of his and shaking it. He smiled warmly at her. Miranda saw the family resemblance immediately. "Don't be a stranger."

"What he said," Kate echoed her husband's sentiments. She stepped forward and rather than just shaking her hand, she embraced Miranda, pressing a quick kiss to her cheek. "Thanks for coming," she added, stepping back. Bryan draped an arm around her shoulders and gave her a little squeeze. Kate looked up into his eyes and laughed softly with pleasure. It was obvious that over the years they had developed their own form of communication.

They completed each other, Miranda thought. She couldn't help envying them, as well as Mike and his siblings. Granted the boys had had to endure losing their birth mother, but by Mike's admission that emptiness was short-lived once Kate came into their lives. From what she could see, the last twenty years had been filled with love and mutual respect.

Miranda was willing to bet that very little silence had occupied those years. When she thought of her own home life, silence had been a main component. Awkward silence, uncomfortable silence, uncommunicative silence.

Soul-sucking silence.

"You're very quiet," Mike noted several minutes into their trip to her apartment. "Are you just tired or did they overwhelm you? They do have a tendency to do that, even if they don't mean anything by it," he confessed.

"Neither." She was too wired to be tired and his family hadn't overwhelmed her, they had thrilled her. Every one of them, including Mike's sister, Kelsey, although she had to admit that at the beginning of the party the youngest Marlowe seemed to be sizing her up, as if gauging her suitability for Mike. "I was just thinking."

"About?"

No one asked questions in her family, even when they'd all been together. They just let things pass and never even acknowledged the silence. Uncomfortable topics were avoided at all costs.

"About how lucky you were," she told him. "And still are."

Slowing down and stopping at a yellow light he could have easily made, Mike looked at her for a long moment. "Yeah, I can think of a couple of reasons to be grateful."

There it was again, the heat that rose whenever she was in his company and the distance between them was less than a yardstick. The physical attraction was becoming stronger and this would cause a problem, she just knew it.

But not if she didn't let it.

"I was talking about your family," she informed him almost primly.

Mike grinned at her, mischief gleaming in his eyes, before he pressed down on the accelerator again.

"So was I." Two beats passed before he added, "Among other things."

Among other things.

She had a choice. She could either ask for him to elaborate or allow it to pass. The latter was the easiest. And the safest. She chose the former. Maybe she didn't want to be safe anymore. "What other things?"

"I'm grateful for my career," he began whimsically, then became serious. "Grateful that I wrote the column that got you so hot under the collar." His voice lowered just a touch. "Grateful that you're sitting here beside me tonight."

Miranda knotted her hands in her lap and stared straight ahead. She couldn't make out a single thing, her mind wouldn't focus.

She wasn't going to get caught up in this, she lectured herself. There was no future. Once he was finished getting what he needed from her father, she knew that Mike Marlowe would become someone from her past, not her present. The less tangled up with him she allowed herself to get, the better off she'd be.

"I have to be sitting here tonight," she pointed out dryly. "You're my ride."

"Why, Miranda Shaw," he pretended to be surprised and hurt, "are you telling me that you're just using me for your own purposes?"

For a second, she thought he was serious. "No, I—" And then she saw the broad grin when he couldn't keep a straight face any longer. "Do you enjoy flustering me?" she demanded.

The grin only widened. "It has its perks." He eyed her appreciatively before looking back at the road. "I didn't know women still blushed."

"I'm not blushing," she insisted, resisting the urge to press her hands against her cheeks.

"Then it's a skin condition?" Mike asked innocently.

"Yes," Miranda answered without missing a beat. "An allergy. I'm allergic to hotshot sportswriters who think they have all the answers. The only way I can keep it under control is if I don't come within fifty feet of one."

They'd reached her apartment complex. Mike pulled his car up into the first available spot he found in guest parking.

"Too late for that," he told her. "Looks as if you've entered the 'danger zone.'"

She was going to ask what he meant, but she didn't get the chance. The very next thing she knew, Mike was leaning over, moving his upper torso to invade her space.

Then his lips touched hers.

And all hell broke loose.

She'd braced herself for that old familiar sinking sensation to take root. That sinking sensation usually so steeped in disappointment she could barely stand it. But if that sensation was even marginally present now, it was masked by the wild rush of her blood and the almost overpowering roar in her ears.

Not to mention the heat. The heat was everywhere, burning into her very soul.

However, it definitely was *not* comfortable, for a very simple reason. She was twisted into him and the driveshaft was between them like a short, metallic old-fashioned chaperone.

But all that was a minor inconvenience. It didn't drive them apart. It certainly didn't keep her from sinking into him.

Her head began to spin.

Miranda realized that she'd threaded her arms

around his neck and that as the kiss progressed and deepened, she tightened her hold. Although Mike's hands were against her back, any second now, in one swift movement of his wrists, his hands would easily form a wrap around her rib cage...and her breasts.

What's more, she wanted him to touch her.

Damn, but she tasted sweet. Sweeter than anything he'd ever had. But then, he suspected that all along from the first moment he saw her. Suspected, too, that kissing her wouldn't be like kissing any of the other women who had come through his life.

Kissing Miranda stirred a hunger inside of him that took more than a little control to tamp down. And even now, he wasn't sure if he was doing it. She made him want to lose his head.

To lose himself in her.

And that was dangerous. Because to get lost in her would mean opening himself to all sorts of problems and complications. And ultimately, he would open himself up to heartache. Most matches did not work out. Most couples, at least those of his acquaintance, didn't go on to "live happily ever after" as promised in the fairy tales. And he would never forget how alone he'd felt, how abandoned, when his mother died. She hadn't left him by choice, but the effect was the same. And then Kate almost left because his father had hurt her, made her feel that he didn't care about her. She hadn't been his stepmother then, just his nanny, but he'd still loved her dearly and had formed a deep attachment to her. Thank God his father had come to his senses quickly enough.

But for the most part, attachments, real attachments, were still difficult for him. The specter of abandonment was too great to risk.

So what did he think he was doing now, falling into a kiss that he himself had initiated?

No harm, no foul, he'd just step away. He wouldn't allow himself to go down that primrose path that led to almost certain danger. He would pull back and pull away. Easily.

In a couple of minutes.

For now, he just wanted to savor this bit of heaven that had dropped into his lap, so to speak, before he scrambled to save his immortal soul and his somewhat more fragile psyche.

Maybe a minute longer than that, Mike bartered with himself. After all, actual loss of control was still down the road. He could stop this in a heartbeat.

If he wanted to.

And he did.

In a minute.

In just another minute....

Chapter Ten

Any second now, she would melt into a puddle. Miranda was certain of it. From the heat of his mouth alone if from nothing else.

Wedging her hands against Mike's chest, she forced herself to pull her head back, to focus. Not an easy feat with her brain spinning out of control like a drunken top.

She ran her tongue along her dry lips. They felt parched. She willed air into her depleted lungs. But when she asked, "Why did you do that?" she still sounded breathless to her own ear.

Because I've wanted to since I picked you up this morning. Afraid of scaring her off, Mike resisted the urge to kiss her again. "I guess I just couldn't help myself."

But Miranda knew better. "You're not the type who can't help himself. You're the type who always stays in control."

With a laugh, Mike shook his head. "As flattering as that is, you're not that excellent a judge of character." He paused for a moment, wondering how personal he could risk getting and what it would cost him if she felt that he'd stepped over the line. Still, while he liked to make the most of opportunities that came his way, he wasn't the type to use them to his advantage if someone would wind up hurt by his actions. It was important to him that Miranda understood that.

His eyes held hers as he spoke. "If you think I kissed you to insure that you don't suddenly make your father unavailable to me—"

She could have sworn her heart stopped beating. "Yes?"

"You're wrong," he said simply. "I'm a sportswriter, not some cutthroat news journalist determined to get ahead at all costs." He'd known a few writers like that and they were not in his circle of friends. "I like what I do and the way to keep on doing it is to earn the respect of people in the business. If you get a reputation for being ruthless, that pretty much shuts a lot of doors in your face. I like open doors."

She believed him. She also believed he could probably sell ice sculptures to the natives in Alaska.

"You do have a honeyed tongue," she told him. It wasn't a compliment so much as an observation. It was time for Cinderella to grab her one remaining shoe and run. Drawing in a long breath, she let it out again. "I had a really great time, Mike." *Far better than I thought I would.* "Thank you for inviting me."

"My pleasure," he told her. Slowly gliding the crook of his finger along her cheek, he added, "Really."

Miranda officially lost count of how many times he'd made her breath come to a screeching halt in her throat, how many times he made her blood rush in her veins. Both seemed to be happening with a fair amount of regularity and with each time, she had less resistance when it came to Mike. Less inclination to follow the path forged by common sense, and more reasons to go with her newly surfacing emotions.

She would regret this, she told herself. She knew that like she knew her own name. And yet, she couldn't help herself. Couldn't keep the words from surfacing on her tongue. "Would you like to come in for…something?"

"Something?" Mike echoed, amused.

When he arched his eyebrow like that, it sent tiny shivers along her spine. "Well, the Bedford police really frown on drinking and driving, so I can't offer you a drink."

"You can if I wait until it gets dissipated in my bloodstream."

That meant he'd have to stay awhile, she thought. And every minute that he did was a minute she drew closer to complete meltdown. And surrender. "Think of everything, don't you?"

"It just came to me," he countered. Getting out of his

vehicle, Mike stopped for a second. "I won't come in if it makes you uncomfortable."

Oh, God, did it ever. The very thought made the hairs on the back of her neck stand in rigid attention. But not having him come in made her far more uncomfortable. Or maybe *restless* was a better word for what she was experiencing even at this moment.

She'd been hovering on the cusp of restlessness since she met him.

Rather than debate it, or ask him again, Miranda turned on her heel and murmured, "Come on. You know the way."

He wasn't so sure about that because his current path felt extremely rocky. Unfamiliar. But at the same time, it was exciting picking his way through heretofore unexplored terrain.

Terrain he found himself *really* wanting to explore.

Reaching the door of her ground-floor garden apartment, Miranda fumbled with her keys, dropping them once. Mike bent down to pick them up and as he came back up to her level, the journey afforded him the opportunity for a very thorough assessment of her legs and torso. A number of previously dormant impulses suddenly quickened within him.

Damn, he hadn't felt quite like this since he was a sophomore in high school.

Instead of unlocking the door himself, he handed her back her keys, silently leaving the choice in her hands. He wanted her to know that she was not without power in this situation. That actually, she had *all* the power. She could still change her mind, still send him on his way if she wanted to. He wanted to be sure she under-stood that the ball was in her court and that he wasn't about to steal a shot.

Unlocking her apartment door, Miranda walked in-side. He was half a beat behind her. Switching on the light, he closed the door and flipped the lock. Sealing them in and everyone else out.

The sound of the tumblers falling into place echoed in her head. Miranda ran her tongue along the inner edges of her lips. Why was she suddenly so nervous? It's not as if she'd never made love to a man before.

"I promised you a drink," she heard herself saying, "but I'm not sure I actually have anything." The people she entertained—but infrequently—all drank some form of diet soda. "I can take a look in the fridge. Maybe you'll get lucky."

"I already have," he answer softly, catching her hand before she could run off into the kitchen, "And you don't have to bother rummaging around. I'm not really thirsty." His eyes slowly swept over her face, all but making love to it. There went her air supply again, dis-solving into nothingness. "Not for a drink."

How could he do that? How could he turn her knees into tiny melting ice caps with just a single look? What was she, thirteen?

"What are you thirsty for?" The loaded words some-how found their way out of her ultra-dry mouth.

This time, Mike didn't answer her. Instead, he gently took her face between his hands and lowered his mouth to hers. And kissed her so hard and so long, she was cer-tain that her soul came to life.

She sighed, completely and utterly captivated, as he drew back to look at her.

"Is that better?" he asked.

That snapped her out of it. Miranda watched him in stunned confusion. Was he asking for an assessment of his technique? Had she misjudged him so completely? Was he one of those swell-headed men who thought they were God's gift to the female population after all?

"Better?" she repeated incredulously, barely contained contempt filling her mouth.

"Yes. The first time we kissed, there was a driveshaft all but piercing your rib cage," he reminded her. Amusement curved his mouth and she was certain that he'd read between the lines and knew what she'd just thought.

Embarrassment came and went in the blink of an eye. It didn't stand a chance in the face of the erupting desire taking hold of her.

She wanted to kiss him, kiss his smile until its imprint became one with her. Until she could taste it every time she ran her tongue along her lips.

God, she'd never felt like this before, like some moonstruck teenager clutching a picture of her idol to her chest.

With effort, she tried to talk herself down. Tried to remember that she was on the road to nowhere. Mike kissed far better than she'd even imagined and that was a huge plus, but deep in her heart she knew that he couldn't live up to her anticipation when it came to lovemaking. It was just going to be a bigger letdown *because* of the way he kissed. That just gave her false hope.

If she had an ounce of sense in her head, she would back away now, tell him she'd made a horrible mistake and very politely ask him to leave.

But she was fresh out of sense.

And all she wanted right at this very moment was to have Mike kiss her again just like he had the last time. Kiss her until there was nothing and no one but him.

It was a tall order and she knew the man couldn't fill it.

Until he did.

The moment his mouth captured hers, the excitement came rushing back in spades, throwing the whole world off-kilter. Making absolutely every part of her body ache for him.

He kissed her over and over again, his mouth effectively making love to hers until there wasn't a single drop of resistance left within her—if there really ever had been any to begin with.

This was happening way too fast.

The thought beat like a faint tattoo in her brain. She wasn't that kind of a woman, the kind who made love on the first date. This wasn't even a date, for God's sake, it was research. Research into his background, into the kind of person he was and into the lives of the people who were partially responsible for the man he had become.

Reason failed her.

It never even stood a ghost of a chance. Because all the logic in the world couldn't effectively stand in the way of what she really wanted right now. And what she really wanted was to make love with him—even though she knew that it would be anticlimactic to the expectations that his kisses had generated.

She kept waiting to be disappointed. And while she waited, Mike effectively succeeded in rocking her world. Not once, but over and over again.

One kiss flowered into another and, as with a teakettle that was beginning to boil, the intensity within her body just grew and grew, threatening to blow the lid off everything.

She felt reborn.

All the other times, even in the middle of making love, she could diagram every movement, every step. The anticipation that *this* time there would be starlight and magic would quickly vanish into nothingness, leaving her secretly wishing that the "event" was over with and sadly wondering what in heaven's name was wrong with her and why couldn't she feel what other women supposedly felt?

She was braced for disappointment.

It failed to materialize.

Making love with Mike didn't take the edge off what had been her almost involuntary heightening of anticipation, just *knowing* something wondrous was about to take place. A marvelous sensation flared deep within her core, telegraphing messages to every part of her. It kept growing, enveloping her in agony and ecstasy at what seemed like the same exact moment.

And then, suddenly, an overwhelming eruption touched the sky, then poured down all around her. Her heart raced as she tried her best to keep up, to absorb every moment and make it her own.

Miranda felt as if a tidal wave had swept over her and it was all she could so to keep from crying out his name in wonder. She didn't want him to know she'd never been here before.

The realization that he was feeding on her energy took Mike by surprise. Her pleasure excited him and he wanted to prolong the feeling. He couldn't remember *ever* experiencing this intensity, this overpowering need that left him in awe and made him all but desperate to have this—whatever it was.

Although he wasn't clear how it had happened, they'd made their way from the front door to her bedroom, the path littered with clothing, both his and hers.

He'd begun by shedding his own shirt and then tugging off hers. She'd been the one who almost fiercely unbuttoned his jeans and undid his belt. Mouth sealed to hers, he'd managed to step out of his pants, the thrill of the moment heightening with each wild, erratic beat of his heart.

When they'd finally made it to her bedroom, tumbling onto her queen-size bed, she'd only had on the tiniest scrap of underwear. But even that was too much. He'd eased it off her thighs, then down her legs, as he continued caressing, possessing, letting his hands make love to every inch of her torso the way the rest of him wanted to so desperately.

This was special. *She* was special. He didn't need to be told. He understood that what was happening here in this small, two-bedroom, ground-floor apartment was a first for him.

The fire didn't abate, but raged higher, taking larger bites out of him. Unable to hold back any longer, urged on by the almost wild look in her eyes as he swiftly brought her up to a climax, Mike slid into her, joining with Miranda in every conceivable meaning of the term.

He was going to remember the wide-eyed expression on her face until the day he died, even if that was half a century from now. It made him feel humble and grateful. And ten-feet tall.

Not to mention hungry.

When he began to move his hips, Miranda mimicked the rhythm perfectly, as if they heard the same music, were dancing the same dance. He heard her gasp, either for air or out of excitement, as the tempo increased, taking him with it and thus her, as well.

And then, when the final sensation caught him up in its grip, he clutched Miranda to him so hard, he was afraid he would bruise her. And she, him, because her fingers dug into his shoulders even as her hips rose off the bed, sealing to his.

It took effort not to collapse on top of her. His last bit of strength went into propping himself on his elbows so that she would have some space in order to draw a breath. If she was up to it. Heaven knew he wasn't. He felt as if he would never be able to breathe normally again.

"It didn't come." She whispered the words against his ear but she seemed to be talking to herself.

"What didn't?" he asked, raising his head so that he could look at her. Was she talking about an orgasm? He could have sworn she'd experienced one. His pleasure came from sharing pleasure, from making it happen for his partner, as well, not in gratifying himself. Had he failed her after all?

"Disappointment," she answered when she had enough breath to form the word.

Relieved, Mike laughed softly. Shifting his weight so that he lay next to her, he tightened his arms around her, sharing the aftermath with her. And the afterglow he was experiencing. "Well, it was the *only* thing that didn't come."

Dazed, amused, Miranda stared at him. Her body hummed like a freshly struck tuning fork and tingling sensations raced all up and down her skin. The breath she released sang of contentment. "Is this what it's like?" she asked. "Making love?"

"This isn't your first time." It wasn't exactly a question. He was no expert, but he felt fairly confident that he could tell the difference between a virgin and a woman who'd made love before. There hadn't been the slightest hesitation, the slightest hint of pain, when he'd entered her.

She sighed against his skin and he felt her mouth curve against the skin on his arm. "It might as well have been. I always thought that lovemaking was highly overrated." Another contented sigh followed her words. "God, was I wrong." And then she laughed at herself, locking her arms before her. "I guess I shouldn't be admitting that to you."

In one smooth, swift movement, he shifted his body back until he was over her again. Gazing into her face, Mike lightly brushed her hair away from her cheek.

"Don't worry, this is all off the record. And *for* the

record," he added in a moment of truth that startled him, "you rocked my world, too."

She didn't see how that was possible. He was, after all, an experienced lover. The very fact that he could do this to her meant he had to apprentice somewhere to learn this kind of technique. And his teacher must have really set him on his ear.

Just as he had done to her.

She tried to muster a decent smile. A smile that would veil her thoughts. "You don't have to say that."

A woman who didn't want a compliment. Now, there was a rarity, he thought.

"I know I don't 'have to,'" he acknowledged. "But it is true."

Moved, enthralled and still in the euphoric grip of her very first—and second—orgasm, Miranda wrapped her arms around his neck, raised her head up from her pillow and kissed him. Passionately.

"That's for lying so magnificently," she murmured, just before she kissed him again.

And they began the whole experience all over again.

Chapter Eleven

Another Saturday, another game. So far, they had racked up a month of Saturday and Wednesday games, all with Mike in attendance and still no article had appeared in his column. She'd begun to lower her guard until it was all but gone.

The game was over for today. The Cubs one-run victory had been a triumph for her father's team.

Over by the fence, Mike was talking to one of the other fathers, Tom Anderson. She recalled he'd been the one who had declared himself such an SOS fan during that first meeting. Mike was probably gathering data for the eventual article. Which left her to pick up the equipment that her father consistently brought to each game, a squadron of bats bought with his own money.

"You seeing this guy?"

Startled by the question that had come out of nowhere, riding on a surfboard over a sea of silence, she stopped dead and looked at her father.

"Seeing who?" she asked a tad too innocently, her mind scrambling for an excuse. Twenty-four years old and she was still hesitant to incur his displeasure. It didn't make her happy, but so it goes.

"The guy with all the questions." Steven nodded toward where Mike was standing. "The one with the thousand-watt grin. He doesn't seem to have a kid with him, so I thought he was here because of you."

If only.

The wistful thought caught her off guard. She recovered quickly and played dumb. "He could be here because he's such a big fan."

But Steven shook his head. "Hasn't asked me for an autograph."

She tucked another bat into the over-size duffel bag. Metal thudded dully against wood. Her father, who'd always favored wood, brought an equal number of both kinds of bats for the players to choose from. "Maybe he's a little slow," she suggested.

Her father eyed her for a long moment. She couldn't tell if he was amused or serious. "That how you find him? Slow?"

Miranda caught her lower lip between her teeth. She had a choice. She could revert back to the sedate young woman she'd been and disavow any knowledge of the man previous to this Little League season—which would make her father suspicious about why Mike kept showing up. Or she could bite the bullet and give Mike a working cover by answering her father's question in the affirmative and "admitting" they were seeing one another.

The latter wasn't much of a stretch, really—and technically, not even a lie. They *were* seeing each other—on the field and he *had* come over a couple of times since the night of his family's barbecue.

And each time, they'd wound up in her bed. Her mouth curved almost involuntarily. He had systematically and officially shot down her previously held belief that sex was unrewarding. It was extremely rewarding—with the right partner, she'd discovered and Mike was very, very right.

Miranda didn't fool herself. She wouldn't allow herself to think their connection would eventually lead to picking out china patterns together. It was a magical summer romance inexplicably taking place in February—and if she was very lucky, extending into March. But someday it would be over. She was actually surprised it had lasted this long. At times, it almost made her afraid to breathe, afraid that she'd do something to hasten its demise. However, by the same token, she knew it was inevitable.

But she didn't have to like it.

"No," she finally answered, trying to sound detached. "That's not how I find him." She tried to recall the last time her father had asked her an actual personal question and couldn't. As far back as she could remember, her father had never taken an interest in who she saw…or didn't see, which was more likely. She was his daughter, but he never seemed to see her as a complete person. "But he probably doesn't want to ask you for an autograph because he knows that the great SOS doesn't like to be worshipped up close and personal and I think he's enjoying being around a living legend."

Miranda glanced over her shoulder at her father and saw his face darken like a sky with storm clouds moving along the horizon.

"Don't call me that," he snapped.

"Okay," she said gamely, "a baseball great."

"Or that," he ordered. His voice reverted back to his customary monotone. "I'm just somebody coaching some kids."

She wasn't going to stand by and have her father deny what he'd been. It didn't matter to her that a bunch of pretentious, stodgy men had banned him from baseball. To her he would always *be* baseball.

"But you were one of the best pitchers in the game, past or present," Miranda insisted.

Steven's expression let no one in, not even her. "All behind me now," he told her flatly.

"It's still part of who you were—who you *are*," she said doggedly.

The shrug was careless, the expression utterly unfathomable. "Doesn't mean much in the scheme of things."

His expression might have been bland, but there was a hopelessness in her father's voice. And it broke her heart. Again.

But she knew that arguing with him wasn't the way to resolve anything.

"Why don't I come over later tonight, make you dinner?" she suggested. "You can give Walter the night off and I'll stay over."

Steven looked at her with what might have passed as mild surprise. "On a Saturday night, Randy? A young healthy girl shouldn't have to spend a Saturday night with her old man. She should be out enjoying herself."

It almost made her feel like family again. *I could really love you, Dad, if you only let me in.*

She smiled at him. "Maybe I enjoy spending it with my 'old man.' And who says you're old, anyway?" she challenged.

He didn't smile, didn't rise to the bait the way she hoped he might. "The clock," her father replied, and then he pivoted on the back wheels, turning the wheelchair away from her. "Put those things in the van," he instructed matter-of-factly. "I've got to get my clipboard."

About to volunteer to get it for him, she stopped herself. She knew better. Her father took any offer of help as an insult to his independence unless he specifically asked for it.

So instead she did as her father had requested. Opening the back of his van, she braced herself to pick up the bag of bats in order to haul them inside. She'd only wrapped her fingers around the duffel bag when Mike materialized out of nowhere and took it from her.

"That's too heavy for you," he said, hefting the bag and tossing it into the rear of the van.

Miranda was momentarily amused. By now Mike should have realized that she was a great deal stronger than she appeared. He was just being a stereotypical male. And she had to admit a part of her liked being treated as if she was dainty.

"Is this the part where I go 'oooh, can I touch your muscles?'" she asked in a sugary, singsong voice.

Mike grinned. "That's later, when I get you alone." He winked at her as he shut the doors. "And—" he lowered his voice until it was an unnerving, sexy whisper "—you can touch any group of muscles you want."

He thought he was coming over tonight, Miranda realized. For a split second, she wrestled with her conscience. It pitted visiting her father against being with Mike.

Her conscience won. "About that—"

"Touching a group of muscles?" He grinned.

"No," she said quickly. She might be sleeping with him and having the absolute best time of her life, but he could still make her blush. "I'm afraid I'm going to be busy tonight. I told my father I'd make him dinner at his place."

"Any chance I can wangle an invitation to that?" When she didn't say anything, he figured he had his answer. "I take it this is some family tradition I'd be interrupting?"

"No, not a family tradition." Sometimes, being the good daughter was costly. She was tempted to postpone the dinner. Her father didn't even seem to want her around. It was an instinct to remain steadfast in her decision. "He just seems more down than I've seen him lately." Until today, her father looked as if he was enjoying being a Little League coach.

Mike nodded. "Well, that stands to reason, don't you think?"

She had no idea what he was talking about. "Why?"

"You mean, you haven't heard?"

Her nerves were at attention. "Heard what?"

He supposed he was more tuned in to this, seeing as how he handled all things connected to the sports world. But it had made the eleven o'clock news last night. "Wes Miller died in a boating accident in Miami yesterday."

Her mouth dropped opened. "Uncle Wes is dead?" Shock echoed in her voice.

He wasn't really her uncle, but Wes Miller and her father went way back to the early days of a childhood spent in the poorer sections of Los Angeles. They'd grown up together, shared dreams together and had both played professional ball together. Wes had been catcher to her father's pitcher.

When the gambling scandal broke, Wes had been her father's staunchest defender, but then they had slowly grown apart. She hadn't seen Wes at her father's house in years. She'd had a feeling that her father had pushed Wes away in his desire to distance himself from the game. And to keep the man's reputation unsullied.

Right now, she was having trouble processing what Mike had told her. Wes Miller, dead. The man seemed too full of life to be absent from it. He'd always been her father's complete opposite, outgoing and gregarious. He'd often referred to her father as his "wingman" when they went out. But that had been before Wes and his wife had reconciled, she recalled.

"What happened?" she asked softly.

"Freak accident. He fell overboard and the propeller killed him." The report he'd seen had been far more gruesome than that, going into details he saw no point in sharing with her unless she pressed. She looked far too upset about the man's death as it was.

"Oh, God, no wonder he seemed so lost today." She'd thought something was off with her father. The last few sessions, he seemed to be enjoying himself and then today, she'd noted a regression. Now she understood why. "He probably feels bad because they grew apart after the scandal." She looked at Mike hopefully. "Rain check?"

"Rain check," he agreed without hesitation. "I'll get these things loaded up for you and get out of your way."

Miranda stepped back. As if he could be in her way, she thought.

"What's all this?" she asked later that day as she let herself into her father's modest house. The place could have easily fit into a corner of the house she and her sister had grown up in. But those had been the flush days, before tragedy and scandal had all but sucked her father—and his monetary resources—dry.

She was referring to the three stuffed black plastic bags, lined up on one side of the foyer, just to the right of the front door. The bags leaned against one another like tired commuters in a standing-room-only subway car.

Her father was a minimalist. He disliked clutter and appreciated keeping possessions down to bare essentials. She didn't think he had enough things to actually fill up three bags, certainly not enough things to throw out.

Her father was in the living room. The TV was on in the background, a sports channel featuring a tribute to the high points of Wes Miller's career. "Doing some house cleaning," her father replied, glancing over toward her.

Curious, Miranda reached for the first bag, about to look inside.

Steven lost no time in leaving the living room and wheeling himself into the foyer. "As I recall, you promised me dinner." The reminder stopped her cold. He obviously didn't want her snooping into the bags. Miranda drew away from them. "Don't you think you should keep your word? I'm starving."

No, not like her father at all. She stepped away from the mysterious black plastic bags and picked up the one filled with groceries that she'd brought and momentarily set down.

"Just about to do that," she replied cheerfully, her manner masking her curiosity.

Her father's assistant, Walter, entered. The man was on his way out, whether out of consideration for their privacy or to take advantage of some time off. As he approached her, she nodded a greeting. "Hello, Walter."

"Evening, Miss Shaw," the tall former linebacker said politely. He indicated the bag she was holding. "Need me to carry that in for you?"

"I'm fine," she assured him with a smile.

"But you can throw those out for me before you leave," her father told his assistant, indicating the three black bags.

Miranda noted a small, disapproving frown on the

man's face as he glanced down at the bags. But in deference to peace and his position, he kept his thoughts to himself and merely nodded. "Sure thing, Steve."

She watched him pick up all three bags and heard the faint clinking of items as they shifted.

What was her father throwing out and why didn't he want her looking at them?

She forced the thought from her head as she made her way to the kitchen. Dinner with her father was never something she took for granted.

Miranda found it difficult keeping her mind on the conversation, even though she was the one who had to initiate it. Her father took refuge in silence more than usual, answering in sentences that a three-year-old could have managed.

It was obvious that he was preoccupied. As always, he kept his thoughts, his feelings, inside. Trapped. She gave him a dozen openings in which to say something about Wes's death and he sidestepped them all.

"I'm sorry about Wes," she finally said as she cleared the dishes from the table.

Again, silence initially met her words. And then he shrugged. "People die all the time."

"I can still be sorry about it," she said. "I liked him."

"So did I."

It was a statement. There was no emotion behind it, which bothered her a great deal. Would he sound like that if something happened to her and someone asked ask him about her demise? She didn't want to explore the answer.

"You two were friends for a long time," she said for lack of anything else to say.

He nodded. "Yes, we were."

"Why did he stop coming around?" she asked suddenly. The dishwasher loaded, she closed the door and turned around to face him. "Did you send him away?"

"Things happen," he replied evasively. "Look, I'm kind of tired tonight. I'm going to turn in. You can hang around if you want."

She knew better. "No, I think I'll go home. Need any help?" she offered impulsively.

"No," he said with finality, not bothering to turn around.

"Of course not," she murmured under her breath as she walked in the opposite direction, out of the kitchen and toward the front of the house. "What was I thinking?"

Taking her purse, she crossed to the front door. "Good night, Dad," she called out just before she let herself out. She thought she heard him say something in kind, but wasn't sure.

Miranda tried the doorknob after she let herself out to make sure the door was locked. It was. With a sigh, she headed toward her vehicle in the driveway.

The garbage pails on the far side of the driveway caught her attention. The internal debate took all of three seconds as she strode toward the pails and flipped back the lids. The newly deposited black plastic bags were piled on top of each other.

Loosening the first plastic tie, she opened the bag and looked in. For a moment she couldn't believe what she saw. The bag was filled with baseball memorabilia, things her father had collected or had been awarded over the length of his career. Quickly, she pulled the top bag out and then peered into the second bag. And the third. All three bags contained what she had regarded as her father's treasures.

This had to be a reaction to Wes's death, she thought. No wonder Walter had looked so disapproving. To a sports lover, throwing out this sort of memorabilia was tantamount to sacrilege.

She knew her father had to be a great deal more heartbroken than he'd let on—Wes had been his best friend for years—but she just couldn't let him do this, couldn't let him throw out the visual trappings of an illustrious career.

Quickly glancing over her shoulder as if, any second, she expected her father to come barreling down the driveway in his wheelchair, she took all three bags out of the trash container and loaded them into the backseat of her car.

The entire drive home, she was acutely aware of the bags behind her. It was all she could do not to pull over to the side of the road and start going through them. Had he thrown out everything? She hadn't had a chance to enter his study, where most of the awards and acknowledgments he'd received during his lengthy career were kept. Had he denuded all the shelves, or had Walter done it for him?

Her father had to be *really* upset. For a second, she debated turning around and going back to him, but then she knew she couldn't. She would have to admit to going through the bags and her father wouldn't receive this very well. He valued his privacy too much.

Cut off, held at arm's length, she continued on her way home. The closer she came to her apartment complex, the more excited she grew about the stash she had rescued. She couldn't wait to go through it.

Once she reached her carport, Miranda quickly carried the bags, one at a time, into the apartment. Anticipation mingled with sadness, when she finally tossed her purse on the sofa and sank down on her knees, ready to get down to business.

The doorbell rang before she could untie the first bag.

"Now what?" she muttered under her breath. Disturbed about her father's mental state, she wasn't in the mood to be sociable right now.

Reluctantly, she rose to her feet and crossed to the front door. She flipped open the tiny cover from the peephole and looked out. The question "Who is it?" never made it to her lips.

It didn't have to.

Curiosity, fueled with a fresh, different kind of excitement, had her quickly flipping the lock and tugging the door open.

Mike was standing on her doorstep, an opened umbrella in his hand.

He grinned at her. "Is it raining yet?"

He was referring to their rain check, she thought, laughing. "No, but you can come in anyway." She shut the door behind him. "How did you know I'd be home?"

Mike shrugged, not completely willing to tell her that he'd missed her and had passed by a couple of times in hopes of seeing lights in her window. That would have made him sound entirely too caught up in their relationship for him to admit. At least for now.

"I had to go in to the newspaper to file a column. The way back passes by your complex. I took a chance you were home—and you were." He was about to brush a kiss on her lips when the sight of the garbage bags caught his attention. This was something new. "A little OCD?" he asked. She raised her eyebrows in a silent question. "Obsessive-compulsive disorder," he elaborated. "Kate once treated a kid who liked to surround himself with all his worldly possessions. It pained him whenever his parents tried to throw anything away even if it wasn't his. Having all those things around made him feel secure." It was the *Reader's Digest* version of the disorder, but he figured it got the idea across.

Being a sportswriter, Mike could appreciate more than most how upset she was about this, Miranda thought. "I found these in my father's trash cans." He was still watching her a bit skeptically. "It's filled with his memorabilia. I think Wes's death knocked him for a loop and sent him spiraling into a full-blown depression."

"Could be," Mike agreed. He tugged open the bag closest to him. Framed photographs of the last World Series Shaw had played—and won—tumbled out on the rug. "Wow, this is like a treasure trove." He didn't bother to hide his eagerness. "Do you mind?"

She gestured toward the bag. "Be my guest." Sitting

back down on the floor, she went back to rummaging through the bag she'd originally started to open. "He obviously doesn't care about these things anymore. Or thinks he doesn't," she qualified more quietly.

There were autographed balls, yearbooks dating back to his first season, one of his game-winning gloves and other things a fan could only dream about.

"What are you going to do with all this?" Mike asked.

"Hang on to it until my father realizes that he shouldn't have thrown it all out, that this does mean something." Miranda pulled out a stained envelope. Opening it, she scanned the handwritten letter inside. It was addressed to her father. "That his life means something. And that—" Her heart stopped as the words she was reading sank in. "Oh, my God."

Surrounded with a small army of statuettes, Mike glanced up. "What?"

Miranda didn't answer for a moment. Instead, she reread the letter. Twice. The numb feeling only grew more intense.

Mike shifted closer to her, his curiosity aroused. "What did you find?"

"Nothing," she retorted. She quickly folded the letter as if that could somehow lock in the words and keep them from spilling out. "Something I have to look in to," she admitted. There was a plea in her eyes as she said, "Don't ask me to say more than that yet."

Mike watched her for a long moment. A relationship was built on trust and he was building a relationship. The sportswriter in him was filled with curiosity. The man he was becoming opted for restraint. "Okay."

Because he didn't prod, didn't try to take unfair advantage of their association to discover what it was that had drained—she was certain—the color from her face, Miranda threw her arms around his neck and kissed him. Hard and with all the gratitude that flowed through her veins.

For the time being, the unexpected treasure hunt was suspended as Mike kissed her back.

Chapter Twelve

"Something *is* wrong," Mike said when he finally had enough breath to form a complete sentence. Making love with Miranda was always an utterly pleasurable experience, but this time around was beyond what had transpired before. She'd had such verve and fire, he'd barely known what hit him. Rampaging hurricanes had a calmer tempo.

Nobody made love like that without something goading them on.

Miranda raised herself up on her elbow to look at him, her brow furrowed with concern. "You didn't like it?" she asked. "I can do better."

He was tempted to play with the ends of her hair as strands tantalizingly moved along her breast. "*Nobody* could do better. Trust me, I'm happy." He watched her, trying to gauge her reaction. Trying to fathom what had set her off. "But you were like a woman possessed."

Miranda forced a smile to her lips, willing herself not to think about the letter she'd discovered. Or the secret she'd unveiled.

She trailed her fingers along his torso, her eyes on his. "Maybe you just turn me on."

He tried not to shiver as her fingers played along his skin. "Good to know, but you're running from something." He caught her hand in his, momentarily stilling it. "What is it?"

She sighed. When had he gotten so tuned in to her, to her thought process? Or was this just a lucky guess on his part? She shrugged, her skin lightly moving against his. She did her best to sound as if she didn't have a care in the world.

"Maybe I'm just trying to store up as much of this as I can before the inevitable happens."

He gazed into her eyes. She'd mentioned this more than once, weaving her words together as if they were forming some sort of fence that kept her safe. "You mean us breaking up."

"Yes."

Mike measured out his words slowly. "Maybe we won't."

The odds were against them as far as that happening. It made her sad and she tried not to dwell on it. As much as she'd struggled not to get caught up in him, she had. She was going to miss him like crazy when he wasn't part of her life anymore.

"Everyone does," she told him.

He shook his head. "Not everyone. My father and Kate haven't."

"But your mother and father did," she pointed out. "You told me that."

He'd found out this tidbit by accident when he was around fifteen, which, coupled with his mother's death, had kept him from making lasting commitments. He feared what was at the end of the trail.

But this was different. One month into the relationship that seemed to have a will of its own, he knew what he wanted. He wanted her. He wanted Miranda in his life, not for a day or a month, but much, much longer. Along with that, he wanted her to stop writing obituary notices for their relationship.

"Yes, they did," he agreed. "But just because they did—just because fifty percent of the relationships out there break up, doesn't mean that we have to." He cupped her cheek and felt himself falling for her all over again. "Maybe we're in the fifty percent that doesn't."

Moving so that the top half of her body teasingly covered his, Miranda placed her fingertip against his lips and pressed just enough to stop the flow of words.

"Let's not spoil things by looking at probability tables." Her eyes danced as she wiggled the bottom of her torso into place and felt him respond. "All we've got is the moment and what I'd like to do with this moment is make love with you."

Mike pretended to sigh. "You are a demanding woman, Miranda Shaw."

She laughed, tossing her long, straight hair over her

shoulder, making him think of some kind of enchanted sorceress. "I know."

His blood rushed in his veins as he pulled her down to him and kissed her for all he was worth.

Temptation arrived in many sizes and shapes. His came in the form of a faded, stained envelope.

He was tempted, so sorely tempted, to look through the papers that had upset her so much when he'd arrived at her apartment this evening. Whatever was responsible for their almost frenzied lovemaking was in that letter. And it lay not that far out of reach.

The reporter in him wanted to find out what she'd read that had her so agitated. But the man who had found himself caring for this woman so deeply knew that he would be violating her trust. If she came out of the bathroom, where she was now, and discovered the papers had been disturbed, she'd feel betrayed. Satisfying his curiosity wasn't worth it.

So he battled his demons and remained where he was, hoping she would trust him enough to share what had affected her so much.

And that it would be *soon*.

Miranda waited until the next day, Sunday, before broaching the subject with her father. She wanted to do it in person. However, that didn't keep her from picking up the receiver at least half a dozen times, even dialing his number before abruptly hanging up again.

But she couldn't talk about this over the phone. She had to watch every nuance that passed over his face as he explained his reasons. She needed all the help she could get to understand why. Why her father had done this. Why he had voluntarily turned his world upside down, as well as hers.

So she waited until Sunday morning at nine, waited until after Mike had left her apartment. Waited until she knew her father was awake before she planted herself on his doorstep and asked to be admitted.

She had to knock twice before the door was finally open. Instead of Walter, her father was on the other side of the threshold. Walter was apparently making the most of his time off and, according to her father, planned to be back sometime in the early afternoon.

Walter's absence gave her plenty of time to be alone with him. Plenty of time to ask for and hopefully get a satisfactory explanation.

Now that she was here, in the lion's den, standing before the lion, she didn't know where to begin. Taking a breath, she dove right into the middle of the matter. Five seconds after her father had answered the front door, she heard herself asking, "Why didn't you tell me?"

A beat went by. Steven pulled back his wheelchair, allowing her clear access to the living room. Only then did he ask, "Tell you what?"

She felt like yelling at him, like screaming and demanding if he'd lost his mind. Instead, she managed to control her temper and her voice. But it wasn't without extreme effort. He'd lived with this shame for no reason.

Miranda fisted her hands at her waist. "That you weren't guilty of the gambling charges the baseball

commission had you up on, that you took the fall for
Wes Miller?"

His expression never changed. If he was surprised
that she'd found out, he didn't show it. "Because you
had no need to know."

"I'm your daughter."

"And it was my life, Randy, my decision."

She shook her head. "Why? Explain to me why?"
she demanded. "Why would you admit to something
you hadn't done?"

Steven watched his daughter and struggled with his
answer. Taking the fall wasn't something he had done
lightly or on impulse. There had been a great deal of
thought. Wes had come to him late one night, banging
on his door. Terrified and contrite. And desperate. He'd
listened to the barrage of words that had spilled out and
then done the only thing he could.

"Because my arm was giving me trouble and my
career was almost over. Because Wes still had a few
years left after switching from catcher to right fielder."

Everyone knew that a catcher's knees were only
good for so long and then he had to switch over, if he
was lucky enough to continue playing. Wes had been
one of the lucky ones.

"But you weren't guilty—and Wes was," she insisted, waiting for his reasoning to make sense to her.

He was not about to talk about who was guilty and
why. There was something larger at stake. "Wes was my
friend. My oldest friend," he emphasized. "He had some
faults, but friends don't abandon friends in their time of
need." It was what he lived by. And intended to die by.

"All very noble," she said sarcastically. "But that didn't stop Wes from following the herd when everyone turned against you."

Wes had tried, he'd really tried. But his friend had always been weak. Except for once. "Wes saved my life when we were kids."

It was all Miranda could do to keep from rolling her eyes. She was more than familiar with the story. Two stupid kids, playing on the train tracks. Her father's shoe had somehow gotten caught in one of the railroad ties and there'd been a train coming. Rather than abandon him, Wes worked feverishly and got him free less than a heartbeat before the train came barreling down. It could have obliterated them both, but it didn't.

"And you gave up yours for him," she pointed out, frustrated at the sacrifice.

Steve shrugged, unfazed. "Seemed fair at the time. Besides, Wes had a family to take care of. He'd been having trouble with his wife—that was why he'd been gambling to begin with, to try to win enough money to pay off for all those expensive things she was always buying. And if the scandal had involved him," her father said simply, "his kids would have been devastated."

"His kids would have been devastated," she repeated, astounded.

The confused expression on his face told her that her father didn't understand. "Yes."

"What about me, Dad?" she demanded heatedly. "What about me? What about the way I felt, having the other kids taunt me about my father, the cheat, the gambler?" Those were some of the most awful moments of her life. Her sister was dead, her parents divorced and her mother had recently died. She'd never been so alone in her life. Not even the aura of a phantom father to comfort her. "Did you ever stop to think how I'd feel about that?"

"You were smarter than that. Smart enough not to be affected by what the mindless masses believed. You're not a prisoner of what the fickle public think."

"Maybe not," she acknowledged. "But it still hurt to have them think that of you. Hurt to have you the butt of their jokes."

"Then I'm sorry." Though there was no more emotion in those words than in any of the others, she found herself believing him. "I never intended to hurt you."

While his words were sincere, it would take a while to let go. Right then, she didn't want to rehash more of the past. It mattered more that her father finally get his due—just as she'd wanted him to. Except now, there was no need to persuade the commission or have the public rally. The truth could finally come out.

"Since Wes is dead now, Dad, you're free to come forward and finally clear all this up," she urged enthusiastically.

"No," he said, knocking the pins right out from under her.

"No?" She couldn't believe her ears. Why would he continue to live in the shadow of a lie when there was no longer a reason for him to keep quiet?

"No," he repeated. "Nothing's changed, Miranda. If the truth came out, it would still tarnish his reputation, still hurt his family."

"And untarnish yours," she insisted. How could he want to continue this way? He'd taught her that all a man had was his good name. Wes had willingly taken it from him in order to preserve his own. That just wasn't right. "Look, Dad, haven't you suffered enough? Don't you think it's about time you had a little well-deserved recognition?" She wasn't moving him, she could see that by the look in his eyes. Frustration filled her. She knew how immovable he could be. "Without this stupid ban on you, you can finally be nominated for the baseball hall of fame—and you'd be a shoo-in, you know that."

He folded his hands before him on his lap. "I don't need to be in the hall of fame."

The longer she knew him, the less she understood him. "Maybe I need you to be in it," Miranda told him, exasperated.

"Then I'm sorry to disappoint you."

The note of sincerity in his voice wasn't enough for her. She couldn't stand by and let his inaction continue without doing something. But by the same token, she couldn't go against him. "Dad—"

"Discussion over," he said with finality. "Now, if you'll excuse me—" he turned his wheelchair a hundred and eighty degrees away from her "—arguing with bullheaded daughters always makes me tired. I'm going to take a nap."

"It's nine-thirty in the morning," she called after him. Why couldn't she make him listen to reason?

"Never too early to get a jump start on napping," he answered wryly. "Besides, the doctors want me well rested before the next surgery."

Miranda fell silent. She'd almost forgotten about the next surgery. He'd had so many already. Each time one was performed, there turned out to be more to do. It was like they were trying to put Humpty Dumpty together again and succeeding only marginally. And each time, the doctors told her, there was a huge risk to his system—that the operation might be a success, but that he could die.

"By the way—" he stopped and turned his chair half around to look in her direction "—where's the letter?"

She'd carefully folded up the letter in which Wes expressed his undying gratitude and eternal inability to *ever* begin to pay his friend back for his sacrifice. She placed it back in its envelope, and after resealing it, she'd put the envelope in her jewelry box.

"At home," she answered, refraining from giving him any more details unless he demanded them.

"Keep it in a safe place."

Her father's cavalier instruction surprised her. She'd half expected him to order her to bring it back so he could continue being its guardian—or personally destroy it the way he'd obviously intended when she'd rescued the three bags from the trash.

Was there a hidden message here? Was he telling her in his own subtle way that it was up to her to someday bring this to light?

God, she wished that he'd be more straightforward with her than this. Wished that communication wasn't just a word in the dictionary when it came to her father.

"I'll do that," she said as she let herself out.

As far as she was concerned, nothing had been settled.

* * *

"All better?"

It was all she could do to keep from crying out in startled surprise when she heard the question. Lost in her own little world, Miranda hadn't even seen anyone in the area, much less recognized that it was Mike standing before her door.

Mike bearing gifts. Specifically, a very large pizza box. The moment she smelled the aroma coming from the flat, square box, her mouth watered. It reminded her that she hadn't eaten.

"What are you doing here?" she asked, even as she stood up on her toes to brush a quick kiss on his lips. Preoccupied, she blindly dug in her purse for the keys to her apartment.

"Delivering your lunch and waiting for you." She unlocked the door and entered. He followed right behind her, closing the door with his elbow. "You know, I wouldn't have had to stand here, getting some very suspicious looks from some of your more curious neighbors if I had a key to your place," he said, placing the pizza box on the counter beside the sink.

He'd already given her a key to his apartment, a key he'd noted that she hadn't made use of yet. But, nonetheless, the significance behind the gesture was still there. He was willing to share his life with her, but she apparently wasn't willing to share hers with him yet.

Dropping her purse on the floor, Miranda grabbed a handful of napkins and put them on the small kitchen table. "I keep forgetting to make you a copy."

"Give it to me." He decided to bait her and see if she backed off. "I can swing by the hardware store right now, and get a copy. Two if you want—"

She stopped him before he continued. "No strings, remember?" she reminded him. She took two soda cans out of the refrigerator and placed two glasses next to them. "That's what we said."

Sitting down, he drew one glass and one can over to his side. "That's what you said and I let it go because, at the time, it sounded like a good deal." He popped the top. The ring broke off, sliding down his index finger. "It doesn't sound like that anymore. Speaking of 'more,' I want it. I want more than just a casual, two-ships-passing-in-the-night thing." He'd put off saying it, thinking that he'd instantly regret it. Up until now, he'd been commitment-phobic. But the words were out and there was no feeling of constriction, not in his throat, not in his chest.

"It's broad daylight," she answered flippantly as she reached up in the cupboard to take down two plates.

Before she realized it, Mike was right behind her, his body shadowing hers. She could feel his heat. Stirring her.

He took the plates down for her, handing them over. "You know what I mean."

Miranda took a long breath. It didn't help. "I know what you mean." And there was part of her that warmed to the idea—and part of her that was scared out of her mind. "A lot of other guys would be thrilled with the no-strings policy."

She was right. A lot of guys would be. And he would

have been among them. But not anymore. "I'm not a lot of other guys."

She touched his face lovingly. "Don't you think I don't know that? Don't you think that I don't know how special, how different you are from the other men I've come across?"

His frustration levels rose. He could all but hear the "but" in her voice. "Then what's the problem?"

She was honest with him. She owed him that much. "I'm just afraid that if I say it out loud, if I agree to a commitment, it'll be the beginning of the end." She looked into his eyes, hoping he would understand. "That you'll suddenly change your mind and leave."

His mouth curved. It was all he could do to keep his hands off her. "I really don't think that's going to happen."

"You don't *think*—" She emphasized the crucial word, the word everything hinged on.

He realized his mistake. Mike caught her by her shoulders before she could turn away. "Okay, I *know* that's not going to happen."

She shook her head. "My parents didn't get married thinking they were going to get divorced. But they did. And they'd turned away from each other way before that."

The sadness in her voice tore at his heart. But he saw through her, even if she didn't.

"That's not the problem, Miranda. They turned away from *you* and you're afraid you're going to wind up being that little girl standing all alone in the foyer again, your heart in your hand—"

She didn't want to hear it.

"Pizza's getting cold," she said abruptly, trying to shrug off his hands on her shoulders.

She didn't succeed. "But I'm not."

Trapped, she watched him for a long moment. Everything he'd said was true, but that still didn't help her make that final leap, the one that magically took her from her mountain peak across to his. The space was too wide for her to attempt, even though the reward—if she succeeded—was great.

There was only one way to make him drop the subject. She needed a diversion.

"The hell with the pizza," she murmured, throwing her arms around his neck and bringing her mouth up to his.

To sate the appetite that rose up within her, she needed to touch him far more than she needed pizza.

Chapter Thirteen

Her father's revelation continued to eat away at Miranda. She carried it inside of her. It was part of every minute she inhabited, making her preoccupied and stealing away her usually keen focus.

It took less than half an hour for Tilda to notice she was distracted. Her best friend commented on it once or twice, then, not getting any enlightening feedback, she wisely left it alone.

What's more, it stood like an eight-foot barrier, complete with a 360-degree overhead beacon, swirling around, between her and Mike. She was torn between loyalty to her father and loyalty to the man who seemed to accept her better than she was able to accept herself.

And even her loyalty to her father could be split in

two equal pieces, further complicating her quandary. Part of her wanted to do as he asked, to keep silent about the secret she didn't feel was worthy of the effort. The other part of her, the part that belonged to the little girl who worshipped the ground he walked on, felt that her father deserved to have his name cleared and to receive the honor that was due him.

It tore her into little, unmanageable pieces and caused her to lose more than a fair amount of sleep. And if that wasn't enough turmoil for her to deal with, her father was going in for yet more corrective surgery to his spine. She tried not to worry, but it was like trying not to breathe. Doable in principle only, not in reality.

To her surprise, rather than appoint one of the squadron of fathers who faithfully showed up game after game to handle minor tasks he might toss their way, her father turned the responsibility of temporary coach over to Mike.

Miranda wasn't the only one who was surprised. Mike was stunned, as well, not to mention he felt ill-prepared for the job, if for no other reason than that he had no offspring to contribute to the game.

Rather than admit that as his defining argument, Mike began with a technicality. "I'm flattered, Mr. Shaw, but shouldn't you check with someone that it's all right?"

For the most part, these last ten years SOS had gone his own way, listened to his own rules. Sticking to someone else's just didn't interest him.

"I'm the only one I need to check with," SOS told him. "And it's because you call me 'Mr. Shaw' that I'm doing it. You don't follow me around, picking up everything I come in contact with to either keep as a souvenir, or sell on that damn, blood-sucking eBay everyone's so hot over." He paused, looking up into Mike's eyes. "I'm not stupid, Mike. I know who you are and I appreciate the fact that you haven't been pumping me for an interview."

He'd had Walter type Mike's name into a search engine a couple of weeks ago and reams of Mike's columns had jumped out at him. His first reaction was annoyance. But that gave way to curiosity and he'd read several of the articles. And found himself, for the most part, agreeing with what he'd found written down.

Steven's eyes held his for more than just a moment. Mike felt as if his thoughts were being x-rayed. "I want you to be honest with me. Have you been using her to get to me?"

"No. But aside from the fact that I'd never do that, you're not giving her enough credit, Mr. Shaw. Your daughter is much too sharp to allow herself be used by someone else."

And then, having said his piece, Mike was privy to one of Shaw's rare smiles. It came and then went, fading quickly like the last embers of twilight. Going so fast that he almost thought he imagined the whole thing.

"I think so, too," Steven told him. He'd already gone over the fine points of his strategy for the next few games, the rest he expected Mike to have absorbed by hanging around him. "Okay, whatever you don't recall, ask Miranda. She's kept track of everything. Got a good head on her shoulders."

As far as he knew, Miranda had never been on the receiving end of a compliment from her father. "Maybe you should let her know you think that."

Steve shrugged away the suggestion. "She knows," he asserted.

"Still, won't hurt to make sure."

Steve moved on, ignoring the direction the conversation had taken. "Things go well," he told Mike, "I'll be back in a few weeks. Just in time for the play-offs—" he leveled a deep, penetrating glare at his substitute "—if you don't screw things up."

Despite the fact that it was only a Little League game, Mike felt as if he'd suddenly been given a mandate. "I'll do my best not to," Mike promised.

Satisfied, Steven nodded. "And if, for some reason, I don't make it back to the playing field," he continued matter-of-factly, as if he was talking about the weather changing and not his own death, "write me a nice obit."

So, the man *was* thinking about his mortality, Mike realized. "Don't let Miranda hear you talking like that," he advised.

Steven thought of his daughter, of the way she just plowed ahead no matter what life threw at her. She was resilient and he was proud of her for that. "Miranda will be fine."

The man actually believed that, Mike realized. How oblivious could you get? Just because the man was a baseball god didn't mean that he was all-knowing when it came to other matters. Certainly didn't mean he wasn't blind to what was in front of his nose. "You don't know, do you?"

Steven scowled as his eyebrows drew together. "Know what?"

"That you're her whole world," Mike told him, watching the man's face for some sign that maybe he did. "That you always have been. And that she felt completely devastated and abandoned when you turned away from her."

Indignation rose in his deep blue eyes, but Steven kept his voice low, not wanting to attract anyone's attention. He'd always been one who wanted to travel under the radar. The aura generated by success had never sat well with him. "I never turned away from her."

"When your other daughter died—"

Steven's face darkened. It was obvious that he had no desire to go to that part of his past. "Leave it alone, boy."

But Mike dug in. This was for Miranda and the air needed to be cleared, if not by Miranda and her father, then by a third party. He appointed himself. "She needed you then."

"I was *grieving,*" Steven insisted through clenched teeth.

Mike didn't back away. "So was she," he pointed out. "She lost a sister, someone from her generation. Nothing brings mortality closer to a kid than to have someone around their own age die."

Steve said nothing for a moment, then sidestepped the conversation that was not to his liking. He nodded at the duffel bag that Mike had just finished filling with baseball bats that had been used during the game. "Don't forget to bring those with you for Wednesday's game."

With that, Steven applied his gloved palms to the wheels, turned sharply and pushed his wheelchair toward the parking lot.

Mike watched him go, shaking his head. The former pitcher and MVP never looked back.

If she consumed another damn drop of coffee, she was in immediate danger of either floating away or overdosing on caffeine—quite possibly both.

But she needed something to do, needed something to occupy her hands. Flipping through magazines wasn't doing the trick. Her nerves were wound up so tightly, she was afraid she would tear those pages out, shredding them into tiny bits.

Any minute now, she was going to scale the walls.

The surgery wasn't supposed to be taking so long. None of the other surgeries had gone beyond three hours. They were approaching hour number five.

She couldn't take much more of this.

"Want some company?"

Miranda swung around the moment she heard his voice behind her. With a cry of relief and frustration, she threw her arms around his neck. Hugging Mike for all she was worth. Burying her face in his chest.

Right now, there was no room for pretense. She couldn't pretend that she was the independent, completely-devoid-of-strings woman who'd indicated more than once that she didn't need anyone.

She *did* need someone. She needed someone to hold her. She needed him.

"Oh, God, yes," she all but sobbed against his chest.

"Careful," he warned, drawing back. Trying to hold the bag he had brought with him, the one she'd almost squashed, still. "I brought you coffee."

She felt her empty stomach lurch and then all but pull into itself. A wall of nausea rose up at the mere thought of a cup.

"Don't give it to me unless you want me to throw up on you," she countered.

"Fair enough." Taking the container out of the bag, he set it to one side, then took out a second container. She assumed it was a cup of coffee for him until he said, "And also chicken soup."

Now that she could handle. She felt the knot in her stomach loosen. Miranda picked up the container with both hands. "Oh, bless you."

Mike grinned. "One out of two isn't bad. Fifty percent again," he noted just loud enough for her to "overhear." Gently, he guided her over to one of the sofas in the room, then tugged on her arm, getting her to sit down beside him. "I'm sorry I couldn't get here sooner. Major computer glitch at the paper. Hard drive crashed big-time. I had to recreate my column from scratch in time for the next edition. So did a lot of other very unhappy writers."

She nodded her head in mute sympathy, even though her thoughts were elsewhere. She threaded her hand through his. "I'm just glad you're here."

"So how's he doing?" Mike knew it was a loaded question, that if her father had taken a turn for the worse, it would be painful for her to say anything at all. But to skirt around the situation would make it seem as if he didn't care.

Miranda blew out a ragged breath, as if that could somehow put a barrier between her and the oppressive fear she was feeling. The fear that was, even now, growing into almost unmanageable proportions.

"I'm not sure," she finally said. She dropped her arms to her sides. "It's supposed to be a three-hour surgery. Four, tops."

He was aware of what time the surgery was scheduled to begin, but maybe they had gotten started late. "How long has it been now?"

"Almost five." Her voice cracked. The strain of the situation was getting to her, Mike noted. "I can't get anyone to talk to me."

Nodding, Mike rose from the sofa. They'd talk to him, Mike thought. He'd always had a way of getting people to open up—and not resent him for it. "Wait right here."

But she caught his hand, fear momentarily getting the better of her. No news was good news—at least for now. "Just stay here and hold my hand."

The smile he gave her was filled with compassion. Sitting back down, he threaded his hand through hers and gave her a tiny squeeze. "I can do that."

Miranda willed herself to relax. It didn't work. She leaned her head against his shoulder, drawing on his strength.

"I'm really worried, Mike."

He slipped his other arm around her shoulders and softly kissed the top of her head. "It'll be all right," he promised her—praying that he wasn't lying to her.

She knew he couldn't give her guarantees like that.

She tried to cling to it anyway. "I don't know about that," she whispered. "It's as if he thinks he's not going to survive this one."

Mike sensed she wasn't telling him everything. "Why, what makes you say that?"

"He said he loved me." Even as she told him, her eyes filled with tears. "He's never said that before."

He thought of the loving home he'd come from and felt for her. Things would have been a lot different, he knew, if Kate hadn't come along when she had. "Maybe he just realized that he should."

She shook her head. "No, I think the doctor told him something my father wouldn't allow him to tell me. Dad's very big on privacy."

He wouldn't let her go there. There was no point in dwelling on the worst until it came into being. "Maybe this surgery is just making him realize he shouldn't leave things unsaid, that's all."

Her father wouldn't have reached that conclusion on his own. It wasn't in his nature. And then it hit her. "You said something to him, didn't you?"

Mike knew she wouldn't believe him if he lied, but he wanted to minimize his role in this. "You mean, did I tell him to tell you that he loved you? No. But while he was going over what he wanted me to do as coach, he gave you a compliment. I just said that maybe he should tell you that instead of me. He said you knew and I told him it never hurt to make sure." He smiled at her. "I guess he listened."

Miranda brushed her lips against his cheek. "Thank you."

He winked at her. "Anytime."

Impulse slipped over her. Or maybe it was the need to set things right once and for all. It took her less than a heartbeat to finally make up her mind. She talked quickly, before her courage flagged and sealed her lips.

"How would you like to have the scoop of the decade?"

He thought he knew where she was going with this—and for now, he was going to have to decline, even if she could have managed to pull it off.

"You mean, an interview with your father? One of the last things he did was thank me for not asking him for one—he knows who I am."

Maybe her father had known that when he'd told her about Wes. Maybe that had been his covert way of saying he wanted to finally have the truth come out. "No, not an interview. My father isn't guilty of the charges brought up against him."

What would it feel like, to have someone that loyal to him? Shaw didn't realize how lucky he was. "Miranda, I know how you feel and you have changed my mind about your father. *He's* changed my mind about him. I'm going to do what I can to have the commission overlook the offense and—"

But she shook her head. "No, you don't understand. I don't mean he shouldn't have that offense held against him, I'm saying he actually didn't do it." She saw sympathy come into Mike's eyes. "I'm serious, Mike. I've got proof he wasn't the one gambling."

He tried to make sense out of what she was telling him. More than anything, he wanted to believe her. Not because it involved Shaw, but because it involved her. Because it meant so much to her to clear her father's name.

"Are you telling me that someone framed your father?" he asked.

"No, I'm telling you that my father took the fall willingly."

That didn't make any sense to him. Who willingly set himself up for censure, to be banned from a game he loved more than anything in the world?

"Why would he do that?"

Miranda realized that she'd gotten up and was pacing. She had yet to stop being angry over this. She knew her father had been noble to do what he did, but all she could think of was what it had cost him. "To protect someone who meant a great deal to him. Someone he felt he owed his life to."

Mike eyed her incredulously as the words penetrated. "Wes Miller?"

Miranda swung around to face him, surprised. "You know the story?"

Mike nodded. "I did a lot of research on your father—especially when I started coming to the Little League games." But all that was beside the point right now. Getting up, he crossed to her. "Are you telling me that Wes Miller was the one who was placing the bets on the games?"

"Yes."

"And you know this how?" he asked, already piecing a column together in his head. "Your father told you?"

"Yes."

The word of the wronged man. It wouldn't fly, he

thought, frustrated. "It's not that I don't believe you— or your father. I do, but the press sees that as just hearsay."

She played her ace card. "I have a letter as proof."

The old cliché "Stop the presses" echoed in his brain. Mike grabbed both of her arms, bracketing her between his hands. "There's a letter?"

"From Wes to my father, dated shortly after the whole thing went down. Wes pledged his undying gratitude and loyalty for my father's sacrifice—Wes's words," she emphasized.

This was too good to be true. "You've seen it? You've seen the letter?" He tried not to sound eager, but he couldn't help himself.

"I *have* it," she informed him. She expected Mike to all but do handstands over the information. Instead, he looked almost somber. Was she missing something? "What's wrong?"

He thought of the man currently in the operating room, possibly fighting for his life. He didn't want to betray Shaw's trust merely for a scoop. "Getting this letter out to the public, is this what your father wants?"

The question took her aback for a second. Miranda's smile was tinged in sadness.

"Got to know him pretty well, didn't you? No, it's not what he wants," she admitted. "But it's what he deserves, what he's earned. If that letter doesn't come to light, he's not going to get the proper recognition. The only footnote my father'll ever get will be in the minus column."

He agreed with her. "And you want me to be the one to 'break the story'?"

"That's the idea," she confirmed. "That's what you do for a living, isn't it, write about what's going on in the lives of sports figures?" She studied him for a moment. "You know, I thought you'd be a lot more excited about this."

"Oh, I'm excited, all right." And it was a rush, being on the cusp of something so big. But there was the other side to consider. "But you also dropped one hell of a dilemma in my lap. I do this story, he gets his well-deserved recognition, but he cuts me dead for being the one to bring the story to the public's attention."

It didn't take a rocket scientist to guess what was bothering Mike. "And you'd rather hang out with him than be hanged by him."

He nodded. "Something like that."

She tried to think of other options. "I suppose I could hold a press conference." She hated the attention, but there didn't seem to be another way.

"I don't want him turning on you."

That, to her, was already a given. "He'll know I gave you the story."

"Not necessarily. He knows I'm seeing you. I could have rifled through some papers, come across the letter by accident—and run with it. I can always say that an anonymous source gave me the material. It's possible if someone broke into his house—or yours."

But she heard only one thing. That he was willing to cover for her—with nothing in it for him. "You'd do that for me?"

He inclined his head, tucking his arm around her and holding her close to him. "You'd be surprised what I'd do for you."

If the truth be known, Mike was rather surprised at the lengths he would go to in order to protect her and promote a better relationship between her and the father she adored. The father who adored her, as well, but hadn't a clue how to show it.

She smiled up at him. "I'm glad I know you, Mike Marlowe."

He grinned and winked. "Right back at you." For more reasons than she could count, he thought.

"So, you want the 'scoop'?" she asked, having come full circle.

He knew she was determined to clear her father's name. Knew he could help her, though it would probably cost him. "Yes," he told her, "I want the scoop."

"Okay, I'll get you the letter. And I'll tell my father that it was my idea."

"No," Mike said firmly. "I'll only run the story if you tell your father that I took the letter when you weren't looking."

But she shook her head adamantly. "I won't lie like that."

"Okay, say nothing." He kissed the top of her head. "I'll do the lying."

The debate was temporarily tabled because her father's surgeon chose that moment to walk in. He was still wearing his surgical gown and his mask was hanging at half-mast around his neck.

Miranda instantly stiffened like a lightning rod.

Chapter Fourteen

Darryl Reese was an orthopedic surgeon who specialized in matters concerning the spine. He was also a tall, somber man, given to pregnant pauses. The surgeon waited until both Miranda and Mike had crossed to him, giving him their undivided attention, before he began.

"The operation was successful," he told them. "We did what we set out to do both orthopedically and neurologically..."

The pause was unnerving. If everything had gone according to plan, wouldn't he have said so? Wouldn't he be trying to manage some semblance of a smile? Miranda felt that giant knot tightening again in her stomach.

Summoning her courage, she forced herself to ask, "But?"

As she waited for a response, she clasped Mike's hand, vaguely aware of the fact that hers had turned icy.

"However," Reese continued, measuring out each word as if to test its ability to stand alone, "your father has slipped into a coma."

Mike saw Miranda turn pale. "But this happens sometimes, doesn't it?" he asked the surgeon. He was sure he'd read several accounts where the patient didn't immediately regain consciousness. Sometimes, it even took more than twenty-four hours. "And the patient comes out of it in a matter of a few hours, right?" Mike prompted.

"Yes," the surgeon agreed. He glanced at Miranda, offering her a cupful of hope. "It's the body's way of shutting everything else down in order to concentrate on recuperating."

She wanted to be optimistic, but it was getting harder and harder to walk that narrow tightrope. "He's never slipped into a coma before," she told the doctor needlessly. Reese was the surgeon on record for all the other surgeries ever since the initial accident had brought her father to Blair Memorial.

His expression softened slightly, as if he understood what she was going through. "Every operation is different."

"So he *is* going to come out of it," Mike interjected, focusing on the positive for Miranda's benefit.

"The odds are—"

Miranda shut her eyes. Every time someone resorted to talking about odds, she immediately knew that they wanted her to be prepared for the worst—just in case. She suddenly felt very drained. "My father's never been very good at beating the odds, except on the playing field."

She was aware of Mike slipping his arm around her shoulders. Or had his arm been there all the time since the surgeon had entered the lounge? Again, she felt conflicted. She wanted to absorb Mike's comfort, lean into his body. But her survival instinct warned her to be strong. Strength came only if she didn't allow herself to be vulnerable.

She drew away from Mike.

For a moment, he let her withdraw. "Then think of this as a giant playing field," Mike urged.

She saw Dr. Reese nodding in agreement. He was feeling sorry for her. It was talk, all talk meant to comfort her for the moment. But the big picture was that each of her father's operations had carried a risk factor. He'd made it through the other five, getting a little better each time. But maybe his luck had finally run dry.

She felt sick. She wanted to run. She stood where she was.

Crossing her arms in front of her, holding in the growing panic, she murmured, "Right." And then asked, "Can I see him?"

Reese nodded. "As soon as he's out of recovery, I'll have a nurse come and get you."

Miranda's nerves mounted. She hadn't had a good feeling about this surgery, especially since her father had postponed it twice. It was almost as if he'd known he wasn't going to survive.

Oh, God.

She looked at Reese, silently demanding the truth no matter what it was. "He's not going to die before he gets out of recovery, is he?" Her voice sounded oddly tinny to her ear as she asked the question.

"No," the surgeon replied firmly, "he's not. The surgery *was* a success," he reminded her.

So then why is my father in a coma?

She bit back the question. The surgeon seemed confident enough about this last prognosis, but it might have been solely for her benefit. No way could he actually give her a guarantee about her father's condition and they both knew it.

"He's going to be all right, Miranda."

Miranda blinked and realized that she must have zoned out for a moment. The surgeon was gone from the room and the lounge was empty. She and Mike were the only ones in it. Mike was feeding her platitudes.

She was panicky. And she wanted to be alone. As alone as she felt inside right now. She didn't want Mike here. He just represented another heartache down the line and she'd already had too many. It was much easier for her to be by herself, taking care of her father.

"You don't know that," she told him, her voice made hoarse by the trapped tears in her throat.

"The surgeon said the operation was a success," Mike reminded her.

He didn't get it, she thought angrily. "But my father's in a coma. That's not very successful, is it?"

He took no offense at her anger, seeing only the hurt in her eyes. "He'll come out of it."

Miranda almost broke. "Do you swear?" she cried, clutching at the front of his shirt. "Do you swear he'll come out of it?"

Because he knew she needed to hear it, despite how irrational it actually was for him to make the promise, he nodded. "I swear." But when he tried to take her into his arms, Miranda surprised him by pushing him away.

"You can't swear," she struggled to keep from shouting. "Because you don't know he'll come out of it. Nobody knows." Tears began to fall. She wiped them away with the back of her hand but she wasn't fast enough to stem their flow. Her emotions were barreling over peaks and valleys. "He really didn't want this surgery, you know." She'd been the one who'd had such high hopes for it, hopes that he would regain at least some feeling in his lower extremities. "Said it was just hacking away at a numb tree stump—"

"When he first had his accident," Mike interrupted, "the doctors said he'd be paralyzed from the neck on down. And with each surgery, he kept proving them wrong. With each surgery, a little more of him came back to life."

She took a deep breath, then let it out slowly in an effort to regain her control. "You do do your research, don't you?" There was a touch of sarcasm in her voice.

He tried not to let it bother him. Why wouldn't she accept his help? Why wouldn't she lean on him? "No," he contradicted, "I knew that before I started my research. That's just the fan in me."

"I thought you said that you were too disappointed in him to stay a fan."

"I lied," he admitted. "Oh, I was disappointed in him, but as I got older, I realized that things weren't just black and white and that adults can do bad things without being bad."

She nodded, only marginally aware of what he was telling her. Her mind was crowded with so many memories, so many things she wanted to tell her father. So many things she was afraid he might never hear her say.

The sense of loss inside of her grew almost oppressive. And with it came fear. Not just the fear that her father would die, but the fear that anytime she opened herself up to hope, she ultimately opened herself up to grief and heartache. She couldn't stand it.

It was only a matter of time before Mike left, too. She might as well rip off the Band-Aid quickly rather than wait in anticipation of the pain.

"You know," she began slowly, her voice distant as she tried to numb herself. "You don't need to stay here. There's no telling how long it'll be before they take my father to his room."

Mike shrugged casually. "I've got no place else to be."

Something inside her rebelled against the sympathetic look in his eyes. Rebelled against all the feelings that being with Mike had stirred up. Feelings that led to attachments. And attachments led to heartache because inevitably, in her case, abandonment was never far behind. Just once, she needed to be the one who broke things off, who walked away.

"If you don't mind," she told him almost stiffly, "I'd like to be alone right now."

Mike caught himself thinking that it hardly sounded like her. Something was wrong and he wanted to be there to help when she needed it. "I do mind. And I don't think you should be—"

"What you think doesn't matter," she retorted. "This is my father, my pain, my call. I don't want you here, I want you to go, do you understand? Go. Leave. Now," she insisted when he neither made a response nor a move to do as she asked.

At a loss, all he could think was that maybe he'd been right in the first place, maybe for him relationships just didn't work and there was no point in trying. He didn't need this. And she obviously didn't want him there.

"Okay," he agreed finally, "but I'll check back in with you."

Her face was hard, removed, as she answered, "Don't."

"Have it your way." Turning from her, Mike walked away.

She knew she'd never see him again and almost cried out to get him to stay. But that was only postponing the inevitable.

She didn't cry until she was sure he was really gone.

It was Day Five.

Day Five of what seemed like an endless vigil that had no end in sight. Miranda sat by her father's bed, hoping, praying, sleeping when she could manage to drift off. Her father never opened his eyes, never stirred. With each day that passed, she could feel her heart sink a little more.

Mike did as she requested and stayed away. And

even though she knew she'd been the one to discharge him, she found herself listening for his step, hoping he'd come back anyway. Knowing in her heart that he wouldn't. He was gone for good.

And she felt all the more lost for it.

Tilda had brought her a change of clothes and told her that everyone at Promise Pharmaceuticals was pulling for her father. Pulling for her.

Miranda thanked her. She had no idea when she would be back. For now, she couldn't think beyond the borders of the day, but she'd amassed nearly a month of vacation time, hardly taking more than a day here and there. It afforded her a comfort zone.

But what if her father's comatose state continued beyond that? What if it didn't and he just slipped away from her?

She tried to numb herself, to sleepwalk through everything, and failed. She felt searing sadness over her father. And over Mike.

As she sat there, watching the sun enter her father's room and then disappear, she desperately tried to distance herself emotionally from Mike. It was stupid to feel like this about a man she'd sent away. Stupid to feel anything for anyone.

She'd already walked that road too many times, given her heart too many times, only to have it run over as if it was of no consequence.

Ariel had been more than her sister. She'd been her best friend, her confidante, her mentor. Ariel had been her shelter and her light. Until that light had cruelly and abruptly gone out.

Ariel died. And then her parents' marriage died. Followed closely by her mother's equally untimely death.

They'd all deserted her.

And each departure had left scars in its wake, scars from which she didn't think she could ever recover. Scars that made her so afraid of reaching out—to anyone.

Restless, Miranda got up from the chair beside her father's bed and began to pace, the way she did at least several times a day.

Why wouldn't he wake up?

Exasperated, she glanced toward the opened door. One of the nurses walked by, looked in and nodded a silent, sympathetic greeting.

She'd learned the names of the nurses on duty, made it a point to become familiar with the orderlies. Most of the latter turned out to be fans. It helped somewhat. Her father was getting the best care possible. But the coma continued.

When he made his daily rounds, the surgeon gave up trying to talk her into going home to rest. She was relentless in her vigil.

"There might be no change for days. Weeks," he'd emphasized during his last attempt to get her to pick up the threads of her life.

"And there might be—for the worse." She couldn't bring herself to say that her father might die. "And I won't be here."

Dr. Reese tried one last time to convince her. "Maybe it'd be better that way," he advised gently. "Death isn't a pleasant thing to witness."

He'd get no argument from her, but this wasn't about her. It was about her father. And she couldn't desert him, even if he didn't know that she was here. "He shouldn't have to die alone."

Outmaneuvered, the orthopedic surgeon didn't counter her remark, so he finished making notes in the oversized chart and left. Left Miranda to listen to the sounds of the life-support machines as they hummed and kept her father alive.

Left her to listen to the sound of her own heart as it continued breaking.

The rails on her father's bed were up. As if he would fall out. She'd give anything if he would just make a tiny movement. An eyelash flutter, a moan, something, *anything* to indicate that he was still with her. That he would remain with her for a while longer.

"I'm not ready, you know," she said in a hoarse whisper as she moved closer. She took his hand in hers. It felt cold. A sign of things to come? She tried not to shiver. "I'm not ready for you to go. You hear that, old man?" she demanded, raising her voice just a little. "I'm not ready to have you die on me. You've already left me once. No, what am I saying? It was more than once. Not counting all those times you were on the road, away from home, you left me big-time when Ariel died."

Her voice trembled and she took a breath to steady it. It hardly helped.

"I loved her, too, you know. I could have used you. We could have consoled each other. We could have *all* consoled each other." She tried not to be resentful, but it was difficult. "But you and Mom went to your separate corners, corners that had no room for me. And then you left again when you and Mom got divorced. *And again* after she died. And then that awful scandal broke. You didn't even trust me enough to tell me the real story, just pulled into yourself like you always do. Into yourself and away from me," she cried, tears falling freely. "Like some damn turtle." The fact that she'd done the same with Mike hit her with the force of a well-aimed blow. But it was too late to fix things, to undo what she'd done. But maybe she could still reach her father. She looked down at his face.

"But I was there for you after the accident, wasn't I? Even if you insisted on going somewhere far away inside you again, I was there. Even when you're here, you're not here, but I got used to that. I can put up with that. What I can't put up with is losing you, *really* losing you. So you can't die. Do you hear me?" she demanded tearfully. "I'm not giving you permission to die. For once, think about me. Me, Dad, me, I need you. I need you, Daddy. I need you."

She was sobbing now, as she draped her body over the bed, embracing her father. It wasn't easy. There were multiple lines going into his arms, feeding his body, taking away the pain and guarding against any possible infections. She was careful not to disturb any of them.

She didn't know how long she'd been like that, sobbing, holding on to him, when she felt a pair of strong arms lift her, taking her away from the man she refused to allow to leave his mortal shell.

Not wanting to be separated from her father, she fought the strong arms, fought to be released from them. Fought to be able to be independent, to stand alone.

But the arms wouldn't let her loose, to isolate herself in her grief. The arms were strong and warm and loving. They formed her prison but they formed her haven, as well.

When she finally looked up, she found herself looking into Mike's sympathetic eyes.

"I gave you five days," Mike told her, firmly but kindly. "Five days to be an island." Five days in which he tried picturing himself without her and couldn't. "But five days is my limit. I want you back."

Miranda pulled back, wiping her eyes with the back of her hand. "It's not up to you what I do or don't do," she retorted. But even as the words left her mouth, she felt awful for being this angry. And so hopelessly jumbled up inside. Up was down, black was white and nothing made sense to her anymore.

"No, it's not," Mike agreed. He made no attempt to take her back into his arms. "But right now I can hope that I mean enough to you to have you listen to what I have to say. Your father's doctor called me. Said the nurses told him that you hadn't gone home since the surgery. That you weren't eating. Just how long do you think you can keep that up before you wind up in a hospital bed yourself?"

She shrugged. "I hadn't thought about it."

"Well, think about it," he ordered. "What good are you going to do your father if he comes back around and you're the one who falls into a coma?"

"I'm not going to be in a coma," she snapped angrily.

"And you have a written guarantee from God to that effect? Your father thought the same thing and just look at him." Mike gestured toward the bed.

She pressed her lips together, looking at the still form. Was it her imagination or was her father getting smaller? "He's not going to come back around."

Her pessimism took him by surprise. Usually, she was Pollyanna with pom-poms. This was a whole new side of her. One he didn't care for.

"Yes, he is."

But Miranda shook her head. She knew her father. "He doesn't want to. He doesn't think he has anything to come back for. My sister's gone, my mother's gone, his reputation is gone. The person he sacrificed it for is gone, too, so it was all for nothing and he's forced to keep quiet about it, trapped into silence by his honorable word." She laughed shortly. "Ironic, isn't it? His honor cost him his honor."

"You're wrong," he told her. When she looked at him quizzically, he explained, "He *does* have something to come back for. He has you."

She waved a dismissive hand at his words. "He doesn't care about me—not enough to force him to get better. Hell, just to stick around for a while."

"Yes, he does," Mike insisted. She was pacing around the room again. He felt as if he was arguing with a moving target. "Your father told me so."

She wanted to believe that. With her whole heart she wanted to believe that. But she knew better. "You're making that up."

"No, I'm not. A lot of men have trouble expressing themselves to the person they care about. My father was like that—until Kate taught him that he couldn't just feel those emotions, he had to verbalize them."

A hint of a smile curved her lips. This time, the apple *did* fall far from the tree. "You don't have that kind of trouble, do you?"

Echoes of the past echoed in his brain, urging him to be flippant, to address her question as lightly as possible. Because if he told her the truth, he'd be vulnerable. He'd be leaving himself open to trouble. But he was tired of playing it safe, tired of waking up in the morning to find the other half of his bed empty. If he wanted that to change, *he* would have to change.

"As a matter of fact, no, I don't. But I did have trouble allowing myself to feel something. And probably for the very same reasons you did. But you miss out a lot by not feeling," he told her. "And I'm tired of missing out on things."

She pressed her lips together, trying to regulate her tone. Could he hear the tremor in it? "Are you trying to tell me something?"

"Not trying. Succeeding," he informed her. "Whether you want to *hear* me or not is another story."

But suddenly, she wasn't listening to him. Her eyes opened as wide as silver dollars. "Mike—"

He stopped in the middle of what was going to be a long, solemn speech. *Anything* to get her to come around, to see what she was missing.

"What?"

Miranda pointed to her father's bed. "He just moved.

My father just moved." Mike turned around to look at the still figure in the bed. "He moved his toe," she cried, overwhelmed. "I just saw him!"

Mike was already calling for the nurse on duty.

Chapter Fifteen

Holding her father's hand in both of hers, Miranda dropped to her knees beside his bed. Fragments of prayers raced in and out of her brain.

"Dad, Dad, can you hear me? Do you know I'm here? Squeeze my hand if you can hear me. Just a little squeeze. C'mon, Dad, you can do it. Do it for me. Let me know you're still with me."

And then her heart skipped a beat.

She felt it. It wasn't just her imagination.

She turned her head toward Mike for a split second. "He did it, Mike. He did it." Tears slid down her cheeks. "He squeezed my hand." She leaned her head in closer to her father. "Dad, Mike's here, too. And you moved your big toe just now. I saw you do it. Your left big toe. You're going to walk, Dad. You're going to walk again. Right out of here and into the rest of your life. I told you that you would. I told you," she repeated, trying very hard to regain control over herself.

She released his hand and rose to her feet again. Turning to Mike, she gave up trying to stem the flow of her tears. "He's going to be all right, Mike."

Mike embraced her, holding her close to him. For a moment, too overcome with emotion, he didn't say anything at all. And then he kissed the top of her head. "Yeah, I know."

Drawing back, she wiped her eyes and looked up at him. Struggling for composure. "Now, what was it you were saying?"

"That I want back into your life."

In her heart, she knew it was putting off the inevitable, but she was too happy to dwell on the downside. Her father had come around. "I'd like that, too," she told him just before sinking into his kiss.

Maybe I'll be lucky just a little bit longer, she prayed.

No matter how fast he mended, Miranda noted with a smile, it just wasn't fast enough for her father. His surgeons were astonished at his progress, but she wasn't. She knew how stubborn her father could be. He wasn't the type to give up, not when he set his mind to it.

Since her father had come out of his coma, her days had consisted of working and then going to the hospital to remain by his bedside in the evening for as long as she was allowed. Mike would stop by the third-floor room around eight or nine o'clock to pay his respects to her father.

They were getting along very well now, Mike and her father, she noted with pride.

After visiting hours, she and Mike went home. Most of the time, that home was his. Some of the time, it was hers. They were together every night. She found refuge in his arms, even if it was just to be held and nothing more. She felt safe with Mike. And although she tried to warn herself that she was getting far too comfortable with this routine again, far too accustomed to having Mike in her nights and early mornings, she couldn't seem to help herself. Couldn't make herself stop caring. She was in far too deep.

Even when she occupied herself with her father's physical therapy and everything else that went into helping him grow stronger, right in the middle, she'd find herself thinking about Mike. Missing him. Wanting him to be right there.

Loving him—and there was no denying it any longer—had made her strong, not weak. Strong enough to face whatever happened with her father's health because, at least for now, she wasn't alone.

Mercifully, it was all good.

So good that when the Little League season approached its end and the team Mike had been coaching for her father had made it into their own version of the World Series, her father was able to come to the field to witness the last game.

Rather than a wheelchair, which would have been less tiring, her father insisted on using his crutches and walking from the parking lot to the batting cage. It was a short distance if measured in feet. Long if measured in accomplishment. It was slow, painful going and there was hardly a dry eye left amid the adults who silently watched his progress.

Steven Orin Shaw was their very own hometown hero. Even the children on the two teams stopped roughhousing and sensed that they were in the presence of something important. They all watched a man who wouldn't give up approach them.

Led by Mike, applause broke out and swelled until there was no other sound but the thunderous noise of hand against hand in awed homage.

"Hear that, Dad?" Miranda asked, choking back tears as she directed him to a seat.

"I'd have to be deaf not to," he responded gruffly. Attention of any sort usually embarrassed him, but she could tell that beneath it all, he was touched.

She was proud of him. Proud of being his daughter. "It's all for you."

He tried to look indifferent, but failed. Exhausted from the journey that had progressed by inches, he still stood for a moment and scanned the faces in the crowd. As he had at the last winning game of his third World Series victory, he removed his cap and held it above his head, as if both in tribute to the crowd and in acknowledgment of their tribute to him.

Then, very slowly, Steven lowered himself onto the bench, just another spectator who had come to watch his Little League team play—and win.

When the crowd finally settled down, Mike came

over to them and smiled at his idol. "The team's really glad you could make it. They wanted me to tell you that they're playing this game for you."

"Tell them to play it for themselves," SOS replied, then flashed one of his very rare, shy smiles. "It'll make victory sweeter."

Mike nodded. It was all he could do to keep the secret he'd been carrying around for the last few days to himself. The secret that involved SOS and, by association, Miranda. A part of him was uncertain how it would be received, because he had used the information Miranda had given him, the letter that Wes Miller had written to SOS in the wake of the scandal.

He knew that as far as the man was concerned, Shaw would have just left the story buried. But his own sense of justice wouldn't allow Mike to ignore it. He would have gone ahead even if the former pitcher had died. Shaw's surviving the surgery made it that much more imperative that he rectify the wrong that had been done.

Mike threw himself into the game, sealing the secret away for a little while longer.

He couldn't keep quiet another moment.

Steven's pint-size Cubs had played their hearts out for him and they had won. Win or lose, Mike had arranged for a season's-end celebration to take place at a nearby pizzeria. Between him and Miranda, they had managed to coax Steven into attending.

While they waited for the pizzas to come out of the ovens, Mike picked up the microphone ordinarily used by management to make announcements. He had an announcement of his own to make. One that he knew would catch SOS by surprise. Although he'd known about it for a week, Mike had even kept it out of his column until he could tell the man in person. Shaw deserved to be the first to know.

Mike winced as the microphone squawked to life. "Before we start celebrating the Cubs' well-deserved victory, I have an announcement to make about another well-deserved victory."

He saw Miranda looking at him quizzically and his smile widened. If anyone was responsible for this, she was. Not because she'd provided the information, but because her faith in her father had never wavered.

"Year after year, there has been a grave injustice perpetuated in Cooperstown at the hall of fame. Because of circumstances believed to be true at the time, Steven Orin Shaw was barred from being nominated, much less voted in. Those circumstances have since been reviewed and found to be false. The commission in charge of voting was eager to correct their mistake and I now have the honor of informing the greatest living pitcher—" he turned to face Steven "—that, come the end of July, he is going to be inducted into the baseball hall of fame."

Though he was known for his poker face, surprise was evident in Steven's eyes as he turned to his daughter. "You know anything about this?"

Her pulse pounded. If she hadn't loved Mike up to this point, she did now. "No, I swear. I had no idea. But it's a damn good thing."

The expression on her father's face told her that he

didn't share her opinion. "You gave him that letter, didn't you?"

She hadn't lied to her father yet, she saw no reason to start now, even if it would make her the target of his anger. "I wanted him to start a grassroots campaign to get you in—but I wanted that even when I thought you'd done what they said you had."

His voice was low, steely, as he said, "You tarnished Wes's memory."

"Wes tarnished Wes's memory," Miranda corrected adamantly. "He never cared about the game the way you did. He cared about the money. His ex-wife wasn't the only one who spent it like water. So did he. And his kids are spoiled brats who never appreciated him to begin with, so let's not worry about them. Mike covered the funeral in Florida," she reminded him. "He said that only one of Wes's kids showed up—and he'd had too much to drink even before the ceremony took place. Dad, it's time you stopped worrying about Wes and started thinking about yourself." And then she grinned, moving closer to him on the bench as the pizzas arrived. The server placed theirs right in front of them. "Besides, I deserve a father who's in the hall of fame, don't you think?"

Anything he might have said in response was curtailed as suddenly both sides of his table were filled with well-wishers. Getting up, Miranda stepped away to let her father have his moment—the first of many.

And it was about time, she thought.

Scanning the restaurant, she looked for Mike. He stood in one corner next to an old-fashioned pinball machine, and she crossed to him.

"Why didn't you tell me what you were doing?" she asked.

He shrugged, trying to downplay his role. "I wasn't sure if I could pull it off for this year. Didn't want you to be disappointed if I didn't."

Everyone had shifted over to the other side of the room to gather around her father. She nestled in closer to Mike. "I wouldn't have been disappointed. I would have been thrilled that you tried."

"It's not about me," he reminded her. "It's about him."

"But it *is* about you," she insisted. "It's about what a really nice guy you are." She saw him wince as she said the words. "What?"

"Is that what I am to you?" he asked, abandoning all semblance of trying to play the pinball machine. His mind definitely wasn't on the game. "A nice guy?"

"Yes." He looked far from pleased. "Why?"

He quoted the old adage from baseball. "Nice guys finish last."

"Last isn't so bad," she told him. "As in my last lover. And my first."

The furrow in his brow told her that he wasn't following her logic. "How do you figure that?"

"You're the first one who ever counted." All her life, she'd been schooled by example to keep things to herself, never to say too much. And here she was, pouring out her heart to this man. She flushed ruefully. "Or is that admitting too much?"

"Nope, definitely not too much." He glanced over toward her father. A sense of pride and accomplishment filled him. "He looks happy."

"I forgot what that looked like on him." Miranda surprised him by taking hold of his shirt, rising on her toes and brushing a quick kiss against his lips. "Thank you."

He automatically closed his arms around her, drawing Miranda closer to him. He noted that her father was looking their way for a second, and then nodding, as if silently giving his blessing. Mike couldn't have asked for more.

"For?"

"For everything. For managing the team for him, for fighting the good fight for him. How *did* you manage to get him not just considered but voted in?" She'd made it her business to know a little something about the process. "Nomination season was over in January."

"I'd like to thump my chest and say I have pull, but really, once I showed them the letter—and they had it authenticated," he added as a sidebar, laughing. "Not the most trusting bunch of old men. Anyway, once they realized that your father took the fall for someone else and kept quiet about it all this time, despite the cost to him, they couldn't fix the situation fast enough. They actually voted in a temporary amendment and opened up the nominating process for thirty minutes. That's all it took. Your dad got every vote."

It didn't surprise her, but she was in awe because she'd been waiting for this to happen for such a long time, worrying at the same time that if it did come about, her father might not be alive to savor the honor. "Wow."

"Yes, *wow.*" It was easy to see that Mike was directing the single, loaded word at her, not the voting outcome. "Now that I've taken care of this, I'm sending my superhero cape to the dry cleaners." His grin faded and his expression turned serious. Something in Miranda's stomach tightened in fearful anticipation. "With everything that's been going on, we haven't had much time to talk lately."

Oh, God, here it comes. He's leaving. He's tired of me and he's leaving. Why else would he want to "talk"?

"No," she agreed, "we haven't."

And she desperately wanted to avoid a conversation now, but he had her cornered. She might as well face up to what he wanted to tell her. No matter what, she'd always remember him as the man who fixed her father's life—and brought joy into hers.

Miranda raised her chin, bracing herself. "What's on your mind?"

Mike slowly ran his hands up and down her arms, his eyes on hers. "You."

Rather than admit that she knew he was trying to break up with her, that he wouldn't be there anymore to wrap his arms around her, Miranda decided to make this difficult for him. If it was too difficult, she could have him for just a little while longer.

"What about me?"

Mike didn't answer for a moment. Instead, he laughed at himself. "You know, I never prepared for this moment, never thought it would actually come." He toyed with a strand of her hair. "For a guy who makes his living with words, I'm experiencing a strange, over-whelming shortage of them right now."

"We could do charades," she offered, congratulating

herself that her voice hadn't cracked. If she kept him off base long enough, the crowd around her father would disperse and then she'd rejoin him. Mike wouldn't tell her he was leaving her in front of her father.

At least she hoped not.

But Mike was shaking his head. "I don't think you want to remember your proposal that way."

That pulled her up short. "My proposal?" she echoed. "What proposal?"

He pointed out the obvious. "The one I haven't given yet."

Her head began to spin. She wasn't able to process anything he was saying. "What kind of proposal?" she heard herself asking dumbly.

Mike shrugged. "Funny, serious, romantic. Take your pick." He slipped his arms around her again and drew her closer—loving the way they fit together. "In other words, you tell me."

She looked at him, numb. He didn't mean what she wanted him to mean—did he? "Are you...?"

He grinned. "Yes."

A lack of air made her push the words out. "Asking me—"

Mike's eyes crinkled as his grin only continued to grow. "Yes."

"To—" She stopped to get her bearings. "Why are you saying 'yes' so much? I haven't finished asking the question."

"Because I thought if you heard the word yes often enough, you'd repeat it in the right place."

Excited, Miranda took a deep breath. "Then you're going to have to ask me the whole thing."

"Okay, here goes." His eyes were on hers and somehow, the rest of the room with its noise and its tantalizing pizza smells, seemed to fade away. "Miranda Shaw, will you marry me?"

Even though she was expecting it, somehow hearing the words left her completely stunned. "You want me to marry you."

Nerves danced through him, making him uneasy. She could still say no. "Glad there's nothing wrong with your hearing. Not that I wouldn't love you if you had the hearing range of a stone," he assured her.

More new information she was having trouble processing, Miranda thought. Did he realize what he'd just said? "You love me?"

Mike nodded, doing his best to keep a straight, serious face. But his grin kept getting the better of him. "Among other things."

"What other things?"

"I like you. I lust after you. I respect you." He stopped enumerating and looked at her, waiting. "Want more?"

Bursts of sunshine filled her. She was still celebrating that he wasn't looking to break up with her. She grinned, this time lacing her arms around his neck. "I think I already have more."

He arched a quizzical eyebrow. "More than you can handle?"

"No, not that much more. Just enough," she told him. Mike kissed her then, in front of God, the pinball machine and her father. Miranda sighed. "I love you, too, you know," she whispered against his lips.

"I do now." He drew Miranda back to look at her face. His eyes searched it for his answer. "So, will you marry me?"

There was only a tiny bit of her insecurity still alive and well. But it made her uneasy. She needed assurances. "Only if you promise to love me forever."

"Can't," he deadpanned. "But I can definitely give you the next eighty-five years," Mike promised. "After that, we'll see."

She laughed then, realizing that without looking for it, seeking only justice for her father, she'd discovered the love of her life. And it felt very, very good.

"Deal," she told him, just before he kissed her again.

Much to the pleasure of her father, who was watching them from across the room as he signed autographs.

* * * * *

Don't miss Marie's next romance,
THE BRIDE WITH NO NAME,
available August 2008
from Silhouette Special Edition.

*Ladies, start your engines with a sneak preview
of Harlequin's officially licensed
NASCAR® romance series.*

Life in a famous racing family comes at a price.

All his life Larry Grosso has lived in the shadow
of his well-known racing family—but it's now
time for him to take what he wants. And on
top of that list is Crystal Hayes—breathtaking,
sweet…and twenty-two years younger. But their
age difference is creating animosity within their
families, and suddenly their romance is the talk
of the entire NASCAR circuit!

*Turn the page for a sneak preview of
OVERHEATED
by Barbara Dunlop.
On sale July 29 wherever books are sold.*

Rufus, as Crystal Hayes had decided to call the black Lab, slept soundly on the soft seat even as she maneuvered the Softco truck in front of the Dean Grosso garage. Engines fired through the open bay doors, compressors clacked and impact tools whined as the teams tweaked their race cars in preparation for qualifying at the third race in Charlotte.

As always when she visited the garage area, Crystal experienced a vicarious thrill, watching the technicians' meticulous, last-minute preparations. As the daughter of a machinist, she understood the difference a fraction of a degree or a thousandth of an inch could make in the performance of a race car.

She muscled the driver's door shut behind her and

waved hello to a couple of familiar crew members in their white-and-pale-blue jumpsuits. Then she rounded the back of the truck and rolled up the door. Inside, five boxes were marked Cargill Motors.

One of them was big and heavy, and it had slid forward a few feet, probably when she'd braked to make the narrow parking lot entrance. So she pushed up the sleeves of her canary-yellow T-shirt, then stretched forward to reach the box. A couple of catcalls came her way as her faded blue jeans tightened across her rear end. But she knew they were good-natured, and she simply ignored them.

She dragged the box toward her over the gritty metal floor.

"Let me give you a hand with that," a deep, melodious voice rumbled in her ear.

"I can manage," she responded crisply, not wanting to engage with any of the catcallers.

Here in the garage, the last thing she needed was one of the guys treating her as if she was something other than, well, one of the guys.

She'd learned long ago there was something about her that made men toss out pickup lines like parade candy. And she'd been around race crews long enough to know she needed to behave like a buddy, not a potential date.

She piled the smaller boxes on top of the large one.

"It looks heavy," said the voice.

"I'm tough," she assured him as she scooped the pile into her arms.

He didn't move away, so she turned her head to

subject him to a *back off* stare. But she found herself staring into a compelling pair of green…no, brown… no, hazel eyes. She did a double take as they seemed to twinkle, multicolored, under the garage lights.

The man insistently held out his hands for the boxes. There was a dignity in his tone and little crinkles around his eyes that hinted at wisdom. There wasn't a single sign of flirtation in his expression, but Crystal was still cautious.

"You know I'm being paid to move this, right?" she asked him.

"That doesn't mean I can't be a gentleman."

Somebody whistled from a workbench. "Go, Professor Larry."

The man named Larry tossed a "Back off" over his shoulder. Then he turned to Crystal. "Sorry about that."

"Are you for real?" she asked, growing uncomfortable with the attention they were drawing. The last thing she needed was some latter-day Sir Galahad defending her honor at the track.

He quirked a dark eyebrow in a question.

"I mean," she elaborated, "you don't need to worry. I've been fending off the wolves since I was seventeen."

"Doesn't make it right," he countered, attempting to lift the boxes from her hands.

She jerked back. "You're not making it any easier."

He frowned.

"You carry this box, and they start thinking of me as a girl."

Professor Larry dipped his gaze to take in the curves

of her figure. "Hate to tell you this," he said, a little twinkle coming into those multifaceted eyes.

Something about his look made her shiver inside. It was a ridiculous reaction. Guys had given her the once-over a million times. She'd learned long ago to ignore it.

"Odds are," Larry continued, a teasing drawl in his tone, "they already have."

She turned pointedly away, boxes in hand as she marched across the floor. She could feel him watching her from behind.

* * * * *

Crystal Hayes could do without her looks,
men obsessed with her looks and guys who think
they're God's gift to the ladies.
Would Larry be the one guy who could blow all
of Crystal's preconceptions away?
Look for OVERHEATED
by Barbara Dunlop.
On sale July 29, 2008.

Romantic
SUSPENSE

**Sparked by Danger,
Fueled by Passion.**

Cindy Dees
Killer Affair

SEDUCTION SUMMER

Seduction in the sand…and a killer on the beach.

Can-do girl Madeline Crummby is off to a remote
Fijian island to review an exclusive resort, and she hires
Tom Laruso, a burned-out bodyguard, to fly her there
in spite of an approaching hurricane. When their plane
crashes, they are trapped on an island with a serial killer
who stalks overaffectionate couples. When their false
attempts to lure out the killer turn all too real, Tom and
Madeline must risk their lives and their hearts….

**Look for the third installment
of this thrilling miniseries,
available August 2008
wherever books are sold.**

REQUEST YOUR FREE BOOKS!

2 FREE NOVELS PLUS 2 FREE GIFTS!

SPECIAL EDITION®

Life, Love and Family!

YES! Please send me 2 FREE Silhouette Special Edition® novels and my 2 FREE gifts (gifts are worth about $10). After receiving them, if I don't wish to receive any more books, I can return the shipping statement marked "cancel." If I don't cancel, I will receive 6 brand-new novels every month and be billed just $4.24 per book in the U.S. or $4.99 per book in Canada, plus 25¢ shipping and handling per book and applicable taxes, if any*. That's a savings of at least 15% off the cover price! I understand that accepting the 2 free books and gifts places me under no obligation to buy anything. I can always return a shipment and cancel at any time. Even if I never buy another book from Silhouette, the two free books and gifts are mine to keep forever.

235 SDN EEYU   335 SDN EEY6

Name	(PLEASE PRINT)

Address		Apt. #

City	State/Prov.	Zip/Postal Code

Signature (if under 18, a parent or guardian must sign)

Mail to the **Silhouette Reader Service:**
IN U.S.A.: P.O. Box 1867, Buffalo, NY 14240-1867
IN CANADA: P.O. Box 609, Fort Erie, Ontario L2A 5X3
Not valid to current subscribers of Silhouette Special Edition books.

Want to try two free books from another line?
Call 1-800-873-8635 or visit www.morefreebooks.com.

* Terms and prices subject to change without notice. N.Y. residents add applicable sales tax. Canadian residents will be charged applicable provincial taxes and GST. Offer not valid in Quebec. This offer is limited to one order per household. All orders subject to approval. Credit or debit balances in a customer's account(s) may be offset by any other outstanding balance owed by or to the customer. Please allow 4 to 6 weeks for delivery. Offer available while quantities last.

Your Privacy: Silhouette is committed to protecting your privacy. Our Privacy Policy is available online at www.eHarlequin.com or upon request from the Reader Service. From time to time we make our lists of customers available to reputable third parties who may have a product or service of interest to you. If you would prefer we not share your name and address, please check here. ☐

SSE08R

HARLEQUIN®

American ★ Romance®

CATHY MCDAVID
Cowboy Dad
THE STATE OF PARENTHOOD

Natalie Forrester's job at Bear Creek Ranch
is to make everyone welcome, which is an
easy task when it comes to Aaron Reyes—the
unwelcome cowboy and part-owner. His
tenderness toward Natalie's infant daughter
melts the single mother's heart. What's not
so easy to accept is that falling for him means
giving up her job, her family and the only
home she's ever known....

Available August
wherever books are sold.

LOVE, HOME & HAPPINESS

www.eHarlequin.com   HAR75225

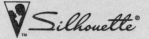

COMING NEXT MONTH

#1915 DESIGNS ON THE DOCTOR—Victoria Pade
Back in Business
Despite their rocky relationship, top-tier L.A. interior decorator Ally
Rogers rushed to Chicago when her elderly mother fell ill...right into
the arms of her mom's meddlesome yet handsome physician, Jake
Fox. Now if only the wily doctor could keep her there....

#1916 A MOTHER'S WISH—Karen Templeton
Wed in the West
Nine years after being forced to give up her son for adoption by
her autocratic grandmother, Winnie Porter wanted a second chance
at motherhood. Tracking the boy down was easy, but his recently
widowed father, Aidan Black, doubted her motives. Would Winnie
make a hurting family whole again?

#1917 THE BRIDE WITH NO NAME—Marie Ferrarella
Kate's Boys
After a late-night walk on the beach resulted in Trevor Marlowe's
heroic rescue of a drowning woman, he took the amnesia victim
in and dubbed her Venus, for the goddess who'd emerged from the
sea. It looked as if she might be his goddess of love, too...until her
former fiancé showed up on Trevor's doorstep.

#1918 A SOLDIER'S SECRET—RaeAnne Thayne
The Women of Brambleberry House
Gift-shop owner Anna Galvez's life was tangled enough—but when a
wounded helicopter pilot rented the attic apartment in her sprawling
Victorian mansion, things really got chaotic. Because Army Chief
Warrant Officer Harry Maxwell was dangerous, mysterious, edgy—
and everything Anna ever wanted in a man.

#1919 THE CHEF'S CHOICE—Kristin Hardy
The McBains of Grace Harbor
To Cady McBain, it was strictly business—hire bad-boy celebrity
chef Damon Hurst to inject some much-needed buzz into the
family's historic Maine inn. To Damon, it was his one chance at
a comeback...and it didn't hurt that Cady was a real catch of the
day...or maybe lifetime!

#1920 THE PRINCE'S COWGIRL BRIDE—Brenda Harlen
Reigning Men
Deciding to go undercover as a commoner and travel the world,
recent Harvard law grad—and prince!—Marcus Santiago soon
landed in West Virginia. But who could ever have imagined that the
playboy royal would be lassoed into working as a ranch hand for
Jewel Callahan...and that the cowgirl would capture his heart in the
bargain?